ff

faber and faber

By Garrison Keillor:

Lentils and You

10 Steps to More Sensitive Writing

Choosing Your Next Waiting Area

Orville the Canadian Goose

Dear Heart: The Correspondence of Eudora Welty
and Weeb Eubanks

Why I Am a Man

Me

by

JIMMY (BIG BOY) VALENTE

GOVERNOR of MINNESOTA

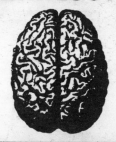

ff

As told to

Garrison Keillor

First published in the USA in 1999
by Viking Penguin, a member of
Penguin Putnam Inc.
First published in Great Britain in 1999
by Faber and Faber Limited
3 Queen Square London WC1N 3AU

Printed in England by Mackays of Chatham plc, Chatham, Kent
Set in Filosofia
Designed by Mark Melnick

Illustrations on pages 11, 80, 94, 97, 111 & 143 courtesy Mark Zingarelli.

Illustrations on pages 10, 16, 17 (2), 30, 31, 38, 53, 58, 65, 77,
83, 112, 116 & 133 © CSA Images.

A CIP record for this book is available from the British Library

ISBN 0–571–20236–5

2 4 6 8 10 9 7 5 3 1

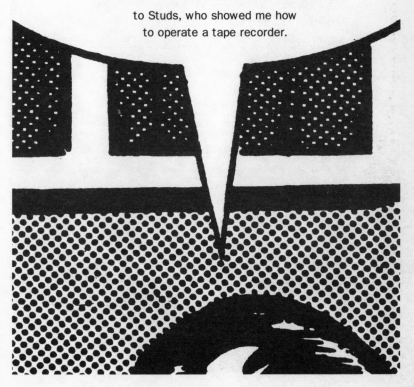

Jimmy (Big Boy)
Valente acknowledges:

this book is for you, baby! *We showed the world.* And for all of my fellow U.S. Navy Walruses. *Loud and proud.* And for my buddies from the wrestling ring. I love yer big ugly mugs. And for all the little people. Your votes were not wasted. And for the women of Viking Press. *Oh Lordy mama mama.*

Garrison Keillor acknowledges:

to Studs, who showed me how
to operate a tape recorder.

Author's Note

This book is a work of fiction, inspired by
a news item of November 1998 in my beloved
Minnesota. The work is satiric, and like most satires,
it works from a few facts, but should not be construed in
any way as an autobiography of an actual governor of
Minnesota, God bless him.

I am grateful to Sharon Mazer, whose *Professional
Wrestling: Sport and Spectacle* (University Press of
Mississippi) was so informative and inspiring.

CHAPTER 1

THE BABY IN THE BLIZZARD

The day of my conception was a pellucid June afternoon in Minneapolis, 1951, and the location was a ten-foot oak table in the Founders Room at the Minikahda Club, where my parents had just nailed the Heffelfinger Cup clay-court mixed-doubles championship 6—4, 6—2. They tossed down a couple gin slings and slipped upstairs and there, on a table where no Jews or Negroes and only one Norwegian had ever sat, they spread themselves out and created a new life. There is a photograph of the two of them taken a half hour or so before, in their tennis whites, holding a silver loving cup at courtside, my father's foot up on the rail of the judge's stand, my mother clutching a racquet to her bosom, and they look so **gifted and radiant and incandescently happy,** it's obvious why they did what they did and put me up for adoption. Their lives were too wonderful to make room for a child right then, especially since they were not married.

He was a brokerage executive married to someone else and she was engaged to his best friend, the heir to a major grocery fortune, and they enjoyed their carnal moment together on the oak table and then dressed and my father washed his face and resumed his marriage.

My mother was twenty. She was home for the summer from **Mount Holyoke.** Her father was the eldest son of a railroad tycoon, and they lived in a red-roofed Creole mansion overlooking Lake of the Isles and she golfed three times a week at Minikahda with the Dayton girls and swam and played tennis. She

My grandfather's house in Minneapolis. I was born in a room on the third floor.

was slender, long-legged, boyish, and her blond hair was cut daringly short. She was a hell-raiser in general. My father, who perished while duck-hunting in 1953 when his waders filled with water, had observed her the week before dive stark naked into the club pool at 1 A.M., on a night when he sat at poolside in the dark, brooding and drinking. On a dare from her friends, my mother walked out of the ladies' dressing room and onto the deserted terrace, dropped her robe at the foot of the diving board, strode to the end of it, and did a perfect half-gainer into the water. My father stood and helped her up the ladder. She thanked him and found her robe and wrapped it around her. "Let's play tennis sometime," she said.

She might have sought out an abortionist and had me pinched off, but she was in the midst of a terrifically entertaining summer and it was easier to ignore me: She was small and didn't look pregnant until her sixth month. In

the fall she returned to Mount Holyoke for her senior year, where she majored in French and was a fencer and in the drama club, and in December, she and her two best friends took the train to New York to see *Come Back, Little Sheba*, and there, one night at the St. Regis Hotel, she looked at herself naked in a mirror and realized she had to confront the fact of my existence.

She telephoned home in the morning and confessed.

She wept. She pleaded for forgiveness. She lied. She told them she had been forced by a friend into having sex and that she could not divulge his name because she had promised not to. She told them that she loved her fiancé and could not bear the thought of causing him pain.

Her family swung into action. A conference was called, emissaries were dispatched to the fiancé's family, negotiations were begun, and by the second week of January, a deal was struck whereby I would disappear, the wedding would take place in April, the groom would be indemnified by a sum of $200,000 for her loss of virginity, and the family would post bond of a half-million to assure her faithfulness for the first ten years of marriage.

I was born in January 1952, in a third-floor maid's room at her family's mansion, in the midst of a Minnesota blizzard, born premature, a puny four-pounder, bald and bug-eyed, too enervated to wail, and was carried by the chauffeur to the black Chrysler and gently laid on the back seat and was driven through the drifted streets of Minneapolis to

University Hospital, where I lay and baked in a glass drum for two months, a feeding tube stuck into the top of my skull, **a free-floating object in the world,** available to anyone for the asking.

I knew none of this until November. A man can learn much about himself by getting elected governor. After November, the press went to work and dredged up the adoption papers and paid off a clerk at county welfare and tracked down my poor old mother and found her in an alcoholic daze at the Minneapolis Club and pumped her for details, and talked to her friends. The day before yesterday that vile guttersnipe Jeff Lundberg of the Minneapolis *Star Tribune* phoned to ask corroboration and comment on it.

That is why I have rushed this book into print.

I want to be the first to tell my own story.

And I want it told 100 percent truthfully, minus those cruel lies that the press tosses in, such as the totally erroneous notion that I was named Josh.

1. I was never named Josh. I was once Clifford Oxnard and now I am Jimmy Big Boy. **At no time was my name Josh.** I am prepared to sue the knees off anyone who states otherwise.

2. I do not live in terror of a man known as The Rodent. He is a deeply troubled man and **I am fully prepared for him** whenever he should make an appearance.

3. I never promised the good people of Minnesota a

one-thousand-dollar tax refund for every man, woman, and child. I only promised the refund if the money was actually there. It wasn't. Had I known the money wasn't there, I wouldn't have promised it. **It's just that simple.**

4. I do not wear a signal ring on my left hand and use it to receive messages from **the planet Ballarat in the Creon galaxy,** though I did once meet someone at the World's Largest Corncob near Walnut Grove, Minnesota, who said she was from there.

5. I do not earn $100,000 a year from the sale of Jimmy (Big Boy) beer. The money I earn is not from the sale of the beer but from the licensing of my name to American Beer Corp., which manufactures the beer. Furthermore, I have a licensing agreement for Governor Jimmy- and Love the Gov-brand action toys, board games, children's clothing, animated feature films, and a planned theme park south of Minneapolis, for which I will be paid a sum in the mid seven-figures plus royalties. **There is nothing in the Constitution that prohibits a governor from licensing his name and likeness.** If people don't like it, they can go get their own licensing agreements.

6. "Big Boy has a collection of German expressionist art in his home in Poplar Bluff worth an estimated $2.5 million." Not true. My success in wrestling permits me to maintain **an excellent lifestyle** but I do not collect German expressionism. Period.

7. I **never** said I would favor the legalization of steroid use by high school athletes and the sale of

hard-core pornography in convenience stores. I only said I thought that we should look into it. There is a difference.

8. I have not "run away" from a match with my nemesis of International World Wrestling, the dreaded Mr. Mashimoto. **Au contraire.** I am actively pursuing it.

9. I have not ruled out a presidential try in 2000. In fact, I have decided to *go ahead* and start organizing my campaign. I will be in the race. **You can count on it.**

These lies were invented by the malicious and despicable Jeff Lundberg of the *Star Tribune*, a hermaphroditic pinhead who needs someone to pick him up by the ears and shake some sense into him. I do not brake for Jeff Lundberg. If I were walking along a cliff and saw him hanging by one hand from the edge, I would get out a nail file and do his nails for him. If I saw him choking on a piece of meat, I would give him a reverse Heimlich.

In this book, I will tell you the truth about Jimmy (Big Boy) Valente as only I can tell it. My childhood as an adopted kid. My reincarnation as a teenager. My Vietnam war experience in the elite Walrus unit of the U.S. Navy. My career as world heavyweight champion of professional wrestling. And my come-from-behind election as governor in 1998.

You gotta love it.

For a professional wrestler with a shaved head and a Fu Manchu to be elected governor of Minnesota—all I can say is, America, I love you. Election Day 1998 was the greatest day of my life. It will be surpassed only by Inauguration Day 2001.

The thought of it makes me toasty warm on these cold winter nights.

I'll be sitting ramrod-straight in my seat on the flag-draped platform before the U.S. Capitol in Washington, D.C., dressed in my black suit and Led Zeppelin T-shirt, a big wad of Copenhagen in my cheek, and on the back of my big bare head I'll feel, like dancing snowflakes, the cold glares from all the **big bonzos** in the seats be-

January 21, 2001: Look for me here, President Big Boy.

hind me and I'll smile my Big Boy smile to the cameras on the platform, and then, after one of those mealy-mouthed **"O Thou Who Didst Once on the Sea of Galilee"** prayers read by

some pathetic dope in a collar, I'll stand and raise my right hand with the World Tag-Team Champion gold ring on the third finger and place my left hand upon the Holy Bible held by my foxy wife, Lacy, and look the Chief Justice **Billy (the Robe) Rehnquist** straight in his black cobra eyes and shift the wad into the left corner of my mouth and vow to **preserve, protect, and defend** the Constitution of the United States and then turn to give Lacy a smooch and hug my daughter, Tiffany, and my son, Adrian, and shake hands with Bill and Hillary and squeeze Al Gore's hand, maybe bear down a little until his eyes water and he looks queasy, and say, **"Tough luck, buddy boy"** and hold my arms up so that my supporters out in the cheap seats can see me and I'll cock my ear to that distant cry of "Jimm-ee, Jimm-ee, Jimm-ee!" and slip my black headband on with **"Mess with the best, die with the rest"** sewn on in rhinestones and turn to go to the limo and look up and see every Senator and Congressman and Justice and ex-President and Ambassador standing, mouth open, in shock and confusion, as if they had just witnessed the explosion of the **Hindenburg,** wondering, How did this happen?

It's called democracy, boys.

The man with the most votes wins, and if you don't think Jimmy (Big Boy) is presidential, then you have got your head where the sun don't shine: You are not thinking democratically. The votes of truck drivers count as much as those of people who read *The New York Times*.

Politicians forget that. They think that getting elected makes them wise and elegant indeed. They sit in their **royal chambers,** wearing their French cuffs, and are addressed as **My Distinguished Colleague** and **My Learned Friend** and go off to a thirty-five-dollar lunch of linguini and shrimp and sundried tomatoes with some lobbyists in blue pinstripe suits who treat their every opinion as **a precious pearl.** And the pols start to imagine that this is true and they forget all about the heavyset folks in the taverns knocking back a beer and bitching about their cars, their kids, their sore backs, and those lying, cheating, butt-kissing, backstabbing bozos they elected to office.

Believability is my biggest asset. Jimmy Big Boy is a guy you would enjoy sitting next to in a bar watching the Vikings pound on the Packers. That is something the voters sense instinctively about me. I would sit there and munch on nachos with you and buy a round when it's my turn and not talk your ear off, not act like we were best pals, and if I said I was going to the can and take a leak and would be right back, I'd be right back, I wouldn't sneak out on you.

Poop magazine ("We Dish the Dirt on the Stars") says that I live in a palatial home, and that, far from being a populist, I am a connoisseur of fine Bordeaux and a collector of art and a fan of Woody Allen.

I am not a yuppie. Take my word for it. I don't collect art or drive a Blazer. I can bench-press 325 pounds. I don't care for fruit. I feel that almost any dish could be improved by putting bacon and melted cheese on it. As for movies, Woody Allen is fine if you enjoy watching videos of other people's birthday parties, but I keep falling asleep. Arnold

 Schwarzenegger is the man. If you want to be the man, you got to beat the man. Woody Allen has never made a movie that can touch *The Terminator*. No comparison. People think Woody Allen can write because he's jittery. That's b.s.

I was elected governor of Minnesota because the people of Minnesota can see through blizzards of b.s. and appreciate common sense. I rode around Minnesota in a rented motor home with **DEFOLIATE IN 98** painted on the sides and raised the flag of rebellion and told the people, **I CAN DO THE JOB AND I AM NOT A POLITICIAN AND I DO NOT LIE.** That was all they needed to know. Using the discipline from my Walrus training and my years in the ring, taking control of the situation, staring the bonzos down, whacking them into their holes, going nonstop for weeks at a time, town after town, rallying the people to the Ethical Party cause, I was beautifully rewarded on Election Night. I stood on the balcony of the Jimmy for Governor headquarters suite at the Lucky Lucre Casino Hotel and leaned over the railing, my arm around Lacy, and yelled, **"GOVERNOR OF MINNESOTA! THAT'S ME, BABY! BETTER GET USED TO IT!"**

I was pumped. I'd been on diet supplements I get from a Mexican supplier, to keep my adrenaline up, and both of us were flying high on brandy Alexanders. Lacy had worn **a black velvet blouse** that always turns me on and an insinuating perfume and I took her in my arms and kissed her long and hard. I think she suddenly liked being married to a head of state. And then I saw the **red rose** taped to the railing.

She was saying, "Well, congratulations, Champ. Now what do we do?"

"Maneuver you into bed and tear your clothes off you," I said, as I inspected the rose. There was a note taped to it that said, "Congratulations from The Rat." I flung it over the railing and it fluttered down six stories to the hotel terrace.

I turned to Lacy. "I have been on the sawdust trail for three months in the cause of statesmanship and now I would like to mix my perspiration with yours," I said. But I was thinking about the note. As I **unbuttoned her blouse,** I made a mental note to get my automatic pistol out of the overnight bag and slide it under the mattress.

"What about the kids?" she said. "They're wide awake and bouncing off the ceiling. They want to be with us. And your supporters are down in the ballroom hollering their heads off."

"Send the children down to talk to the supporters." And she did. When she went in the bathroom to put on her negligee, **I loaded the pistol** and stuck it under the mattress and double-latched the door, and slipped into that king-size bed and made love to her, and when I came up for air, I saw on the TV screen Tiffany and Adrian at the podium, telling everyone **how great their dad was going to be,** and then suddenly

my wife hollered and tossed her head back and forth and writhed and panted and I yelled and pounded my fists against the bed, and that was when I found the second red rose. It was taped to the picture over the bed, one of those fake French landscapes. I leaped up from the sheets and grabbed it.

"Did you come?" she moaned.

The second note said, **"Well? Did you?"**

"THE RODENT!" I gasped.

Lacy tried to pull me back down into bed, but I showered fast and dressed in a T-shirt and running pants, pistol in the pocket, and took an elevator down to the ballroom. I looked everywhere and The Rodent was nowhere to be seen. People were trying to grab my hand, slap my back, buy me a drink, interview me, and I kept looking in dark corners for **a sawed-off slant-eyed pigtailed terrorist** whose avowed aim in life is to cut my jugular vein with his teeth and kill me.

The next morning, I had a headache that went down to my knees but I appeared on every network news show in America and told them that I was the start of the New Wave and to look out. I was the blue-eyed hero, people were talking about me wherever I went. Lacy was photographed for *People* magazine and I was on the cover of *Time*. Jay Leno wanted me. David Letterman called personally. John Travolta telephoned me, and Geraldo, and Joan Rivers and Ricki Lake and Jerry Springer and Cokie Roberts and Donald Trump and Oliver Stone and Al Franken and dozens of others. And I got this terrific book deal. A cool half million to sit and talk about myself. Easy work, if you can get it.

I am not an author so this book is not going to be big on daffodils and Tintern Abbey and the stuff they stuck in our ears in high school English, like:

> I passed—a Field—
> Where Children—Drink
> From Buttercups—of dew—
> I passed—Eternity—I think—
> Or maybe it was—You.

As I told my ghostwriter Mr. Keillor very clearly at the outset, this is not a book where I resolve the issues of **my troubled childhood** or dream about **a world united in peace and harmony.**

GHOST:
Could we go back to your parents winning the tennis tournament?

No. I'm sorry I ever mentioned it.

GHOST:
Are you interested in meeting your mother?

No. I don't care to dredge up the past. It does no good.

GHOST:
It's interesting, though.

Not to me. We are writing this book in **one weekend** at Jimmyville, my little compound on Maui, sitting in the Frangipan Cottage, which is next to Ginger and Bougainvillea, looking west onto the Pacific, drinking vodka gimlets in the great long lanai with the fresh hibiscus that Miyoko cuts every morning we're in residence, the doors wide open to the veranda, and me lying in my water chair, jabbering into a tape recorder, and my ghostwriter sitting in a straight-back chair twitching like **a rat in a coffee can.** What is the matter with you? **Relax.**

GHOST:
I am relaxed.

I did not request this man. I specifically asked Viking Penguin to assign **a California writer,** or a European, someone who could appreciate me as an individual, and I specifically said, "Not a Minnesotan," so who do they send? This **lemon-flavored twitch** from Anoka. Let me tell you: Minnesota is a cold place in more ways than one. **I have always been treated more like a star in other places than in Minnesota.** I went to L.A. after the election, there were fourteen TV crews following me from the airport to the NBC studios to Arnold Schwarzenegger's. **Fourteen.** Minnesota? I get off a plane and everybody looks at me out of the corners of their eyes. They're afraid to show interest. To run up and say, "Wow! You're great! This is fantastic! Can my girlfriend take my picture with you?" People from Minnesota don't do that. **It's not a show business type of place.** Not much sense of fantasy. Very big on equality. They think nobody should ever have to fail and nobody should ever hit it too big. Like my liberal brother-in-law. You call him an elitist and he gets dizzy and has to go lie down. But there is a clear pecking order, and professors and doctors and lawyers and writers are at the top of it, and people like me are at the bottom. That's what grinds my butt. You're a writer. What's so hot about you? Your socks smell as bad as anybody else's.

Garrison

GHOST:
I'm going to edit out the stuff about me.

Like hell you are. For the record, Mr. Keillor is **a tired old hack** with a gecko face and thinning hair and a body like a six-foot stack of marshmallows. He is wearing a corduroy jacket and brown slacks and Hush Puppies. This book is his big break and now maybe he can afford to buy a gym membership and a pair of decent shoes.

GHOST:
Tell me about your boyhood.

CHAPTER 3

BOYHOOD

The Lutheran Children's Home stuffed me with Similac for three weeks and gave me away to Arv and Gladys Oxnard of 42nd Avenue South, Minneapolis, who wanted a little brother for their girls Eunice and Arvonne. They named me **Clifford.**

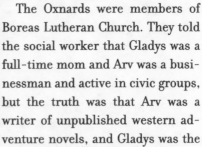

Gladys

The Oxnards were members of Boreas Lutheran Church. They told the social worker that Gladys was a full-time mom and Arv was a businessman and active in civic groups, but the truth was that Arv was a writer of unpublished western adventure novels, and Gladys was the breadwinner. She ran a café on 38th Street, Gladys's House of Lunch, and worked from sunup to midnight fixing tuna casseroles and pigs-in-blankets. Eunice, a short-tempered girl, was left to raise me and Arvonne. Eunice wrote an A on my forehead so everyone would know I was not her real brother.

"You are adopted and you could be sent back to the orphanage at any time, day or night," she said. "All it would take is one phone call from me."

Our house was a big old musty brown stucco house near the railroad tracks along Hiawatha Avenue in south Minneapolis, with a rusted screen porch on the front where I'd hide when big dogs came rumbling around. People let their dogs run loose back in those days, and it scared the piss out of me, especially the neighbors' dog **Bruno,** a giant mastiff with drippy chops who bit first and

Arv Oxnard

sniffed you later. I remember the smell of Lysol every spring and women screaming at their kids and saying, "I am on the verge of a nervous breakdown. I mean it." But mostly I remember big dogs.

The house was dim, being in the shadow of a ten-story linseed-oil plant next door, and it reeked of linseed and Gladys's and Arv's cigarettes. Both were chain-smokers. They kept conch-shell ashtrays everywhere. The furniture was in toxic shades of burgundy and chartreuse and lavender: Gladys only bought furniture when it was marked down at least 80 percent, so she got the dregs.

GLADYS'
HOUSE OF LUNCH
GOOD THINGS TO EAT
OH BOY!
THIS LOOKS
GOOD

Gladys worked at the café, which did a big business among hefty folks who craved hot beef sandwiches, and Arv sat in his lounger chair and read *Reader's Digest* ("How to

Put the Ka-Zoom Back in Your Marriage") and dreamed of earning big money with his western novels. He had about twelve of them typed up and ready to go. His brother Arlen had earned a bundle with a motorized ski he had invented, called the **Snow Zoomer,** and also a radiator that pressed pants, and Arv was smarter than Arlen, so he figured it was only a matter of time.

To get himself in a writing mood, he put on a pair of chaps and six-guns and a ten-gallon hat and went into the basement and swaggered around, yelling, getting the feel of the dialogue, and raced to a typewriter and wrote it all down, things like **"You dastardly chaps had best not trifle with the Cimarron Kid lest you get your comeuppance, as most assuredly would happen!"**

He came up with an idea for a new book about every two months. He'd sit soaking in the tub nipping at the peach brandy and get all warm and happy as the new plot would emerge, shining and brilliant, and he'd start again to set the world on fire. He'd write *The Sumac River Boys and the Missing Mustang* or *Buck and Bob and the Big Smelt Run* or *The Revenge of the Reverend Slim Jeeves* and mail it off to a publisher and a month later it'd come back unread and he'd mope around, tail between his legs, and marinate in the bitter juices of defeat. But he was used to disillusionment, being a Democrat.

The only thing that didn't disappoint Arv was Gladys's hula meat loaf, with pineapple and Kahlua. He chased it with a cherry-flavored bicarbonate and took a nap in the lounger and woke up refreshed and crazy, ready to assault the bastions of publishing again.

Every night Gladys made tapioca pudding for me and sterilized a dozen baby bottles, and all day I lay on the couch with Eunice and Arvonne and we watched shows on an old Dumont television set, hour after satisfying hour. My earliest memories of childhood are laced up with Tarzan wailing in the jungle and Roy Rogers galloping across a river and the Three Stooges falling over furniture. And at night there was wrestling, the Crusher and Killer Kowalski and Mad Dog Vachon and Gorgeous George shaking his fist and yelling at them pencil-necked geeks. When those big boys climbed into the ring snarling and strutting and hurling insults at each other, I sat up and my eyes got wide and I made not a peep. I can't remember anything that preceded them. To me, the world began with roly-poly men grappling in the ring.

I recall a bout between Floyd (Farm Boy) Barnes and Mr. Tojo who both resembled giant infants with their shaved heads and big bellies, toddling toward each other grunting and yowling, bent on infantile goals of domination and possession, and I remember how the Farm Boy screamed when Mr. Tojo rubbed burning sand in his eyes, how the poor man flopped around and wailed and staggered blindly in circles as Mr. Tojo sneered and tormented him, and how true to life it seemed to me—the clueless referee, who couldn't see the burning sand though **six thousand screaming fans** in the Minneapolis Auditorium were pointing it out to him, was so much like Arv, and Mr. Tojo was Eunice, who delighted in bending my arms and legs to see if they would

snap off, and the audience grieving helplessly outside the
ring was six thousand Gladyses, helpless to save me.

Daddy Arv cut my hair with electric clippers and gave me
a trim that looked like I was being treated for lice. The next
step, it seemed to me, would surely be the lunatic asylum. I
begged him to shave it and he gave me a buzz cut. I was six. It
was a turning point.

One Sunday after church I punched Eunice after she
punched me. She was astonished and burst into tears and
called out to Mom Gladys, who called back, "You kids learn
to settle your differences yourselves." **I sneered at Eunice and
poked her again.**

"I'm calling the orphanage right now," she said. "This is
your last day here. They'll come for you in the morning and
you'll live in the orphans' dorm and sleep on a cot, and eat
nothing but rutabagas and rice pudding."

One day a neighbor lady heard screams and found Eunice kicking me in the head. We were playing wrestling, Eunice explained, and she was Eunice the Magnificent and I
was **Cliffie the Biffy.** That was when Grandma Oxnard came
down from Brainerd to live with us. She was a large woman
who looked like Sitting Bull and who woke up every morning believing that **Jesus was returning to earth at about two o'clock
that afternoon,** right after *Days of Our Lives,* and would take
247,000 people straight to heaven and would allow an equal
number to rule the earth. Every morning as she fixed
breakfast, Grandma started to get happy. One day's disap-

pointment did not dim the next day's hope. After lunch, we put on our good clothes, and stood at the stop sign on 38th Street and 42nd Avenue South and as she shouted at motorists I dashed out and handed them little pamphlets that said:

Verily He Cometh Today. Selah.
Before the Sun Shall Set.

The Time For Shopping & Beauty Treatment Is Past, Forget About Lawn Care & Plumbing & The 7 Basic Food Groups, Return To Your Home And Prepare For The Clouds To Part And The Lord Descend On Rays Of Truth And Grace. I Shall Have Sparkling Raiment And A Perfect Body: Will You?

I colored each pamphlet with golden crayons and wrote "Please" in green.

I'd run out and wave the paper at drivers and they'd shake their heads and roll up the windows and Grandma'd yell at them, **"All right, go to blazing hell then! You want it, you got it! Hope you enjoy your eternity, Mr. Know It All!"**

Growing up with Grandma made me skeptical of organized religion, even though she wasn't all that organized. She certainly didn't have much effect on her son.

When I was ten, Arv ran away with the woman who cleaned his teeth at the dentist's, Dr. Nordine's assistant, Fay. She believed in him and his writing, he told Gladys, and she didn't anymore. It had been a calamitous week for him. He went to the library and lost a manuscript in the stacks, a new novel, *Texas Jack in a Real Fix*, and found it two

hours later, and rushed out into a pouring rain and stepped in a pile of dog doodie and dropped his house keys down a storm sewer and a garbage truck drove by and splashed a couple hundred gallons of muddy water on him. Hula loaf couldn't bring a smile to his lips anymore, only Fay would. They went to Fargo, and Arv got a job managing a parking lot. We quit going to Dr. Nordine, an old man who said that the tooth would tingle a little when he drilled, but it hurt real bad. Daddy Arv's leaving did not hurt that bad. Not like a tooth. Gladys poured the Kahlua down the sink and gave his clothes to the Goodwill. He left twelve novels in the basement and she boxed them up and put them in the attic. That was about it.

Grandma only said, "The Lord has dominion over all of us. Nothing happens without His say-so."

She believed that everything was God's will. If she went to the store and forgot her house key and I had to shinny up the rain pipe and crawl in the bedroom window, then God had created the event for a purpose.

Even dogs were part of it. Even Baldies.

The Baldies were a gang at that time. They shaved their heads. They hung around in the park after dark and practiced smoking and slouching. Mainly they loved to sniff glue from a lunchbag and find someone to fight and have a good knock-down, drag-out, eye-gouging, face-scratching, kick-em-in-the-ankles donnybrook. Taste some blood and feel your eye swell up and look down and see teeth on the ground. They had red bruised knuckles from beating up people. They were said to file their canine teeth to razor sharp points, though not the Baldies I knew. They were after my sister Eunice. They told her if she didn't come across for them, they'd break my arm.

She told them she didn't care what they did to me but that if they touched her she'd scream so loud it'd take off the wallpaper. So they came after me. They lay for me on my way home from school, they hid in the doorway of Larson Pharmacy. They wrote in chalk on the sidewalk **TODAY IS THE DAY, WIENER HEAD.** I was scared to death.

I was a regular reader of *Popular Mechanics* and there, among the ads for ventriloquism discs and hernia belts and muscle-building kits, was an ad that said, "Learn Domination in 3o Days or Your Money Back." I sent in fifty cents (what did I have to lose?) and got a booklet that told me I could control others only by learning to control myself.

With the Baldies after me, I had to make like a bunny, and luckily, guys on glue are not so swift, but it was terrifying seeing shaved heads come lurching out from behind garages or doorways. Years later, they were all saved and started an organization called Baldies for Jesus but back then they were strictly evil, and loved to pound on people, and wherever I went, I could hear footsteps behind me.

And then I made a Baldie friend named Tank Baldwin. He was the biggest kid in the sixth grade because he had been held back for a number of years. I became his friend because it made more sense than not being his friend, and he was easy to be friends with. You just paid him four dollars.

Tank Baldwin took care of me, right up to ninth grade, when he tossed a cherry bomb in the teachers' lounge and was sent to Red Wing reform school. For five years, he let it be known that anybody who touched Cliffie Oxnard would answer to him personally and retribution would be swift and sure. Tank was a master of the Indian rope burn and the two-knuckle noogie and the head butt, and in fear of him other hoodlums gave me a wide berth, for which I paid four dollars per month, a bargain.

One day I asked him to show me how to fight. He said, "There isn't anything to fighting. You start out by glaring: you look at the guy like he is Hitler. Next, you get the jump. Always strike first and knock him down. He is surprised by your glare and thinking, **'Hey, I'm not that bad when you get to know me. I'll bet we could be friends,'** and that's when you dive for his legs, or you shove him in the chest real hard. Get him down on the ground, that takes some fight out of him right there. And then you kick him. That lets him know that he's on the street now and there is no referee. He's thinking, **'Hey, why are you so mean?'** and then you kick him again."

Fight hard, fight to win, and cheat. Those were Tank's rules. Today he is one of the biggest car dealers in Minnesota.

I attended Nathan Hale High School ("We never falter, we never fail! We are the boys from Nathan Hale! We are brave and we are young and also we are quite well hung") and was a complete dork, highwater pants and big boats on my feet, and I sniffed some glue (Nathan Hale was nicknamed "InHale High") but not like some guys who wound up so glassy-eyed they couldn't get the paper sacks off their heads. I sniffed only enough to get a little buzz. I needed it to survive those terrible moments when the teacher said, "Mr. Oxnard, would you come to the board and diagram this sentence for the class?" "Mr. Oxnard, would you explain what is meant by 'prime numbers'?" And I would clump up to the front and stand, chopfallen, humiliated, the teacher leering at me, goading me, saying, "What's the matter, Mr. Oxnard? Did you not read the chapter that was assigned for today? Did you forget? Were you too busy, Mr. Oxnard?"

I thought, You old bugger, someday I'll pick you up by your vest sweater and stick your head in the toilet and flush.

I hated every class I was in. I even hated choir. When we sang it sounded like an ancient nomadic tribe keening for their dead. I hated lunch period and the clouds of sickening odors that wafted from the cafeteria. I hated football. The coach of the Patriots was a mickey-mouse freak with a thousand tiny pinprick rules and if you broke one, you had to get down and give him fifty push-ups, and one day I said, "Do them yourself, fish face," and threw my helmet up in the air and quit. I was in drama and was cast as Friar Tuck in a play and had to wear a wool robe and say things like

Behold the blazing chariot of the sun
Spreading like gentle fingers the radiance of his
    heat
O'er leaf-bedizened bough, awakening the fowl,
And causing ferny flower, bush and bud, to open
    wide.

I learned one thing at Nathan Hale and that was loyalty. Even though the school was full of creeps and drips and dumbos and the teachers treated us like scum on a pond, nonetheless I was loyal to Hale and if I went downtown to the Rifle Sport penny arcade on Hennepin Avenue and saw guys in West or Washburn letter jackets (the cool schools) I looked right through them as if they didn't exist. I didn't try to pal around with them. I was no suck-up.

CHAPTER 4

THE NEW ME

When I was fifteen, I went with a buddy, George, to the Minnesota State Fair and we paid fifty cents each to enter the freak show tent, having heard about the Wild Man from Borneo. It was dim and musty in there, and when the two-headed man came out, an old Indian with a gnarly growth on his forehead and a face painted on it, we saw he looked different from the picture on the canvas banner out front. "We've been suckered," George said. Then came a lady with a bad rash (the Alligator Lady) and the Bone-Crushing Anaconda, who was asleep, and the Penguin Boy (*Positively Alive!*), a sullen man with short arms, and we thought of asking for our money back. And then Popeye came out, who popped his eyeballs out of their sockets, one at a time and then in tandem, and the cheerful fat lady Miss Dixie in pink scanties, her voluminous folds stacked like cordwood, and Mr. Chuck Up, who swallowed an orange and then brought it back up, and the Wild Man from Borneo. He was a big brute, a mulatto, well-muscled, with stallion legs and arms like tree trunks, and when the curtain was drawn open on his cage, he **rushed to the front screaming gibberish** and crashed into the bars in a way that made men shrink back and women scream. He seemed **quite satisfied** with the effect he had on people. He **grinned** and **gloated** and thumped on his chest and then picked out a child in the crowd and **leered** at it and bared his teeth and licked his lips until he made it cry. And when the father of the child looked at him in protest, the Wild Man let out a **crazed roar** that sent shivers down the back of your legs, a roar of red-blooded violence and sheer malice.

I went home and practiced that roar in the garage for several days, the roar and the crouched primate stance that went with it, until I got it right, raw, deep in the throat, bloodcurdling, demented.

That fall, I got into deep trouble, and the trouble was what saved my life.

A history teacher named Francis Thawe was giving me the treatment in class, making me stand and look at a bunch of foreign names on the blackboard, asking if I didn't know at least *one* of them, and then he said, **"Think. I know it's hard, but take your time, Mr. Oxnard."** and this got a laugh from all the dewdrops in the class, and then he made the mistake of touching me on my shoulder. I turned, crouched, **and gave him my Borneo roar.**

He was a small slender man in a red-dotted bow tie and tan suit and nobody had ever roared at him before. He twitched like a chicken on a hot plate and he yelped and turned spasmodically, dropping his book, and crashed into his desk, knee first, and knelt down on the floor, and there was a strong odor of urine in the room. Everyone was so quiet you could hear it dripping. He staggered to his feet and his face was drained, which I guess makes sense, and he limped out the door, and the moment it clicked shut, all thirty kids in that class stood up and cheered, even the brown noses. They chanted, "Cliff-ee! Cliff-ee!" as if I had scored a touchdown.

I looked at the love and admiration in their faces, and it was like rain on dry ground. They were proud of me! Girls reached up and patted my shoulder who had never noticed me before. Guys pumped my hand. I got all choked up, I was so happy. Then the principal came and told me I was out of school for two weeks. "It was worth it, Mr Sheffield," I cried. He looked at me gravely.

"This will go into your record, Clifford. It is a blot that you can never erase. Someday a college or professional organization may deny you admittance because of your outburst."

I ran to the front door and turned and shouted so the whole school could hear me, "Freedom! I am free!"

Grandma called Gladys at the House of Lunch and she came straight home with a bowl of chili con carne. She kept saying, "Cliffie, you never did anything like this before. What got into you?"

I tried to comfort her, but I was so proud of myself. It was the first heroic thing I had ever done. It showed me that there was another life for me beyond dorkdom.

I never went back to Nathan Hale. No more choir, no more Mr. Thawe, no girls snickering at you, no haughty women peering over their spectacles at your knucklehead term paper on *Romeo and Juliet*.

What I did was start bodybuilding so I would pass for eighteen and enlist in the Navy and escape from south Minneapolis forever. I saw an ad with a picture of Hank Hercules, "America's Most Coveted Male Physique," that said, "Choose the Body YOU Want!" and underneath—

- ❑ **Big Meaty Thighs & Calves**
- ❑ **He-Man Chest & Broad Powerful Shoulders**
- ❑ **Sinewy Arms with Eye-Poppin' Biceps**
- ❑ **Beefy Mitts with Iron Grip**
- ❑ **A Big Solid Butt**
- ❑ **Large Feet**
- ❑ **Rugged Good Looks**
- ❑ **Powerful Voice**
- ❑ **Hung Like a Horse**

I checked them all, except for **Large Feet,** and sent two dollars to a postal box in Scranton (Dept. 9L), and received back a pamphlet warning against self-abuse and another showing how to fashion a set of barbells from tin cans filled with concrete.

I worked out in the laundry room, eight hours a day, until I barely had strength to lift my head. Every morning I told Gladys I was going to school and snuck downstairs and

I was reincarnated.

closed the door and lay on the floor and pumped iron to the tune of Top 40 hits on WDGY, Wonderful Weegee, and every week recorded my measurements, and in five months, my body was changed into another body. I was reincarnated. From dork to hunk. I built up those sloping shoulders and spindly arms, that concave chest, built 18-inch biceps and a 52-inch chest and a 28-inch waist. My self-esteem shot up. I no longer glanced into mirrors and slunk away; now I lingered and checked myself out.

"What's going on with *you?*" Eunice sneered at me one morning. "You eating Dumb Flakes for breakfast?" I leaned down and with one hand lifted her and her chair up to the ceiling. That quieted her down.

Priority No. 1 was finding the Baldies but they had vanished into the shrubbery. I lurked around the train yard they frequented and could find only one, a small hairless guy we called Boink. He was sniffing glue in a shed. "Cliff, I'm glad to see you," he said. His eyes were big and white!

"Not in a minute you won't be."

"I was never in favor of going after you, Cliff," he said, blinking. "I was the one who protected you. Honest Johnson."

"Nonetheless—" I said, hoisting him up to his feet.

He stood, swaying slightly, his hands in his armpits. "I have been out of the gang for a month now. My hair grows back slowly, but I'm no longer one of them."

"I don't care," I said. I grabbed his collar and shoved him against the shed.

"Before you proceed further," he said, "you should know that I have just enlisted in the United States Marines and that hitting me is a **FEDERAL OFFENSE.**"

As strong as I was I let him go. I was scared to hit him. Those days, I'd open a refrigerator door and pull it right off the hinges. I'd pet a cat and kill it. I didn't want to knock his head off his shoulders.

In August, I enlisted in the U.S. Navy as Jimmy Valente. Because of **Francine.**

She was the new waitress at Gladys's House of Lunch. I had my eye on her for months, and I felt her eye on me the moment I sashayed in the door that morning and perched at the counter. Five months before, she wouldn't have given me a glance, but now she studied me in the mirror as she filled the coffeemaker. I sat tight. I could feel my pectorals swell under my black T-shirt, the biceps fill out the sleeves, the delts and traps and glutes sitting hard and proud. I pulled out a Lucky, tapped it on the counter, lit the match with my fingernail, lit the Lucky, took a drag, let the smoke curl out of my mouth, and inhaled it up my nose. She was watching me the whole time.

Finally she comes over. "What can I get you?" she says.

I say, "A hamburger. Very rare. Cool in the middle. With raw onion. A little mustard." And I take out a comb and I comb my hair back on the sides.

She says, "Okay. No problem."

"Hey," I said. "While you're at it, bring me a glass of gin and a raw egg yolk in a china cup."

"Sure," she said.

She was tall with short black hair and long legs and a short black leather skirt and a pink blouse.

"Pink and black are coming back," I say.

She says, "Oh yeah? Coming back where?"

I said, "At the State Fair, which is where I'm headed, pink and black are truly cool."

Her eyes softened. She said, "I haven't been to the State Fair in years. It's always so crowded."

I said that crowded wasn't a problem so long as you got in the right crowd. I said that I was going to the Beach Boys concert that night. She said that she had always admired their fine harmonies. I said that if she cared to come with me, I happened to have an extra ticket.

When she brought me my order, I tossed back the egg, chased it with gin, ate the hamburger, and put a fiver on the counter.

She took off her apron and put on a pair of cobalt blue shades. "My name is Francine," she said. **"I never did anything like this before in my life."**

I said, "Neither did I. Call me Jimmy. Jimmy (Big Boy) Valente."

"I thought you were Gladys's boy," she said.

I informed her that actually I was no relation to the Oxnards whatsoever.

CHAPTER 5

ENSIGN VALENTE

Francine and I got on the bus for St. Paul and the Fairgrounds on Snelling Avenue. A guy in a cowboy shirt said her name. She ignored him. "He's yesterday's newspaper, nobody to worry about," she said. It was a sweltering day and she felt a little woozy and put her head on my shoulder. He made a smart remark I couldn't quite hear. I turned to tell him to get lost and he was gone.

We got to the fair and strolled around past the Dairy Building and the Old Mill and the Boreas Lutheran Church dining hall, where I could see Eunice filling the napkin dispenser. She knew I had dropped out of school; she said I was a disgrace to the family. How one could disgrace someone like Eunice was beyond me, but it would be fun to try. She was enrolled at the University now and acted like she was the smartest thing since waxed paper. She called herself a feminist and a radical. "If you are a radical" I said, "then I am a radish. You're just a bitter young woman with bad hair."

Francine and I took our seats in the grandstand and sat
through a truly dumb opening act, a weenie folksinging duo
named Trent and Travis, and when the Beach Boys ran onstage and cranked up on "Little Deuce Coupe" she and I
jumped up and danced in the aisle, danced close, bumping,
and she said something about my body that I could hardly
believe, having never heard a woman say it before, that I
was sexy. She wanted to touch my skin, she said. She wanted
to touch me all over.

We were out of the grandstand in two minutes, both of us
hot to get undressed, and we hustled down toward the Midway where I thought we could maybe find a quiet spot between the house trailers behind the freak show tent and
the Harlem Revue. We came to a sort of alleyway between
trailers. In one big silver Airstream, the lights were on in
the front room, people were hooting and laughing. I peeked
in and saw the Fat Lady on a busted red couch and a tattooed
man and Popeye and the ancient Aztec warriors Monty and
Zuma, all of them swigging beer and playing cards, and I
whispered to Francine, "Let's scoot under the trailer,
they'll never hear us, it's the safest place," and we did. We
lay on the grass under the floor where the freaks sat slap-
ping down their cards. I lay facing Francine. I unfastened
two buttons of her blouse and slipped the tips of my fingers
in and touched her secret skin, in the Valley of Dreams. And
then she let out a screech.

She put her hands over her eyes. She said, "Oh my God, I lost an earring! I must have dropped it when we were dancing! I've got to go find it!"

I said, "Francine, I'll buy you another earring, believe me."

She said, "This is an emerald one my grandmother gave me."

I said, "Francine, I would do anything for you but I am not going to go to that grandstand and look around in a crowd of twenty-five thousand people for an earring you dropped."

"All right," she said, "I'll go find it myself. But don't expect me back." And she scooted out from under the trailer and buttoned herself and went marching up the Midway, swinging her arms, mad. She was a girl who knew her own mind. I liked that. I ran after her.

I caught up with her by the dime toss booth. She turned and faced me. "Jimmy, if you love me, you'll go back up in the grandstand and help me find that emerald earring."

I looked at her in her short black skirt and pink blouse and I said, "Francine, I will buy you an emerald the size of a peanut and marry you and we'll live in a house with white columns in front and a swimming pool behind, but I will not go fetch your earring just because you tell me to. A man does that and pretty soon he is wearing a suit and tie and squeaky shoes and living the life of an old plow horse."

We stood in the heat of the August night, the woman of my dreams and me, **in a mist of cotton candy and caramel apples** and the Beach Boys singing about California and the sea and the sun and the good vibrations, but when she turned away and

headed for the grandstand, I couldn't do a thing about it.
She took a few steps and turned around and said, "Jimmy, I
am nuts about your body but I could never go with a man
who wouldn't do a favor for a lady." She walked to the end of
the Midway and through **the arches with their flashing colored lights**
and I saw the guy in the cowboy shirt approach her and they
talked and the two of them headed for the grandstand.

I rode home on the bus and in the morning **I went downtown
and enlisted in the Navy.**

Gladys cried when I told her. "We need you here, Cliffie,
what with Arv gone off. Couldn't you go to the University
and join R.O.T.C. instead?"

I said, "Mom, the U is full of draft-dodging flag-burning
pinkos and pantywaists, and if I set foot over there, it would
be only a matter of hours before I would need to bust a few
heads.

"This is a time for us all to make sacrifices. America's
strategic interests are threatened by Communist-led wars
of so-called national liberation, and if Vietnam falls, Cam-
bodia is next, Laos, Malaysia, Thailand, Indonesia, the
Philippines. The Red Wave could spread to Japan, Korea,
Hawaii, to our very shores—so that what was accomplished
by the G.I. heroes of Guadalcanal and the Solomons and
Okinawa and Iwo Jima will be lost. The blood of our sacred
dead will have been spilled for naught.

"At the U, they learn everything but the most important

thing: that sacrifices must be continually made if the flame of freedom is to remain lit."

She cried some more and then she did what she always did when she was upset, she whomped up a big meal of pork roast and mashed potatoes and corn on the cob and a lime Jell-O salad. Eunice and Arvonne sat silently on the other side of the table, and I ate heartily. I felt bad about Francine though a little relieved that the earring had come loose; otherwise, I might be a daddy right then.

Eunice wore a T-shirt that said **A woman without a man is like a fish without a bicycle.** I pointed to it and said, "Why is it that the girls who don't wear bras are always the ones who nobody cares if they do or not?"

She ignored that. "You're going to Vietnam," she said, "and you're going to burn villages and kill women and children, all because the President of the United States is afraid to admit a blunder."

I said, "Eunice, if I am fortunate enough to be called to serve in Vietnam, I will carry out my mission, which is to preserve the freedoms of you and your dope-smoking pinko pals. If that's a blunder, then America is a whole series of blunders."

"I wish you kids liked each other more," said Gladys. "I swear I don't know where I went wrong."

I packed my duffel bag that night, and in the morning I was on a bus for San Diego.

CHAPTER 6

GUTS

Wearing a dog tag that said **JIMMY VALENTE** I went through basic training and was accepted for the Navy's exclusive and top-secret **WALRUS** program (Water Air Land Rising Up

Suddenly). I was scared they'd stick me among the half-wits in the clerical program, **NARWHALS** (Never Around When Alarm Sounds), but I impressed them with my determination and dominant personality, and they sent me to Walrus Academy at the old Republic movie lot on Ventura Boulevard in Los Angeles, to train on the sound stage where John Wayne romanced Maureen O'Hara in *The Quiet Man* and led his men in *Sands of Iwo Jima*. The sand was still there, and a bronze plaque marked the spot where Duke lit the cigarette and was killed by a sniper. It meant a lot to us **shavetails** to be able to train there.

Walruses were trained to **swim underwater** and **use explosives** to blow up stuff and **run thirty miles** with full field packs

through knee-deep muck and to **swing by rope** over a pond full of ravenous alligators and climb a fence topped with razor wire. We were trained to **stomp snakes** and to take a stick away from a big dog and to **pee straight up in the air** so it is soaked up by leaves on trees and can't be sniffed by enemy bloodhounds. We learned to **live off roots and berries** and rodents and squirrels and to prepare them to make nutritious meals and what kind of leaves make the best toilet paper and which can be used for floss. How to **camouflage** yourself so you can't be detected by the wiliest adversary sixteen inches away from your face. How to use an ordinary table napkin and **tie a man's wrists** with it and use it to gag him. How to **navigate** unfamiliar terrain without directions of any kind. How to modify a man's behavior and sharpen his cognitive skills by poking him in certain places. How to **speak in code** using few words. How to **avoid venereal disease** by using raspberry jam and sauerkraut juice. We were taught to **walk like a man** and display a rugged demeanor. A Navy surgeon gave us chin clefts. We were taught to **drink a bottle of gin** and then chew off the neck and spit out the glass. We were trained to know **the darkness of the human heart.**

It was in Walrus training that I shaved my hair. I wrote to Mom that it was to reduce drag when I swam underwater with a satchel of dynamite in my teeth, but the truth was that I was starting to go bald, and shaving was the best cure for hair loss.

At the end of our three months of training, we were is-

sued our combat fatigues, green and orange stripes with blue plaid pants. It was felt, the CO told us, that clashing colors disoriented the enemy.

I stood up. "Excuse me, sir, but—"

And my buddy Arnie, from Brooklyn, New York, grabbed my sleeve and pulled me down. Arnie was smart. He knew L.A., where to find girls, good restaurants, valet parking. "Avoid trouble. That's the first principle in the military," he whispered. "Go along with the mickey mouse. The officers are idiots but don't tell them. We'll swap these clown suits for olive drab when we get in country."

"You men are the cream of the crop, the top of the line, the state of the art, the best of show," cried the CO. "Very few men in Uncle Sam's Navy have the guts to be Walruses, but you men do. You have Walrus guts, and for that I salute you." And he barked four times, the Walrus signal of recognition, and we all threw our tusks in the air and slugged each other hard on the shoulder, and ran twenty miles to Sunset Boulevard and got smashed on a special drink called The Bombardier, two of which would make you yodel like Jimmie Rodgers and also it killed red ants, and after six of them apiece we roamed Hollywood, overturning cars, starting brushfires, painting "Walruses Rule!!" on overpasses, using our unique skills of subterfuge to avoid detection.

The next day, we were shipped to Vietnam.

We left L.A. aboard a cargo plane that developed engine

trouble and ditched in the South China Sea and we had to ditch, forty Walruses bobbing in the water and no land in sight, but that plane was hauling a load of a **thousand weather balloons** and helium cartridges, and we got enough of them out of the wreck to give ourselves four apiece and fasten them to a life raft and we took off, **each Walrus in an airborne raft** under a cluster of giant olive balloons, and we sailed into Da Nang on an easterly wind, landed on the beach, and strolled into the main mess hall as cool as could be, **forty big men,** tanned, with shaved heads and cleft chins and wearing headache colors. A mess sergeant tried to shanghai us for K.P. I shoved him aside.

"If you're friendly forces, I'd rather meet some enemies," I said.

The entree was Spam in tomato sauce. "Eat hearty," said the CO. "We're shipping out at oh-sixteen-hundred hours."

CHAPTER 7
A DAY IN VIETNAM

It was time to do what we came to do. At oh-sixteen-hundred hours two minutes, five armored personnel carriers took us into the steaming stinking jungle. One minute I was staring at the marquee of the base drive-in (Lola LaSalle in *Teen Sex Vixens, Part 2*) and the next minute I

couldn't see six feet in front of my face. Bugs flew in my eyes and mouth, sweat poured down my face. Only the low woofs of my fellow Walruses kept me from panicking.

In my unit was O'Connell the boxer from Brookline who was reading Albert Camus and Rodriguez the kid from the east L.A. barrio who hoped to become a priest and Cohen the wise guy from Cleveland who had concealed his bad heart murmur by humming during physicals and Jennings whose east Tennessee drawl concealed a swift mind indeed and the company goof-off Johannesen who joked to conceal his fear perhaps even from himself and Milosczewski the first-generation immigrant with something to prove about Polish bravery and Postlethwaite the Yale grad who had the brains of a wet tennis shoe and was always asking if a flush beat three of a kind. And the CO, an Annapolis guy, who went by the rules until Vietnam taught him different.

Suddenly a Walrus barked three longs and a short from the vehicle behind ours, and I dove over the side and into a thicket of briars and grabbed a VC cadre in black PJs and pried an explosive from his wiry fingers and hurled it into the trees and a half-second later came the explosion, a **KER-WHAMMMM** followed by the **WHUMP-WHUMP-WHUMP** of VC mortar fire.

Suddenly AK-47 submachine guns spat fire from all around us. I crawled to cover and the VC crawled next to me. The rest of the Walruses followed and a moment later the personnel carrier went up in a burst of flame. "You save my rife," the VC whispered. "Now you forrow, I read you to safe prace."

"Guess I don't have much choice but trust you," I muttered. "But if you double-cross me, Victor Charlie, you've got a one-way ticket to the People's Republic of Hell, you atheist midget." He nodded. I barked to the other Walruses and they fell into line.

"Where we going, Big Boy?" asked Johannesen.

"We got some butt-kicking to do," I replied. The CO was in shock, unable to give orders, so I did. "Walruses halt and do makeup!" And we reached into our bags and applied the **camouflage paint.** (I took a vow that I would drink a pitcher of warm spit rather than disclose the secrets of Walrus subterfuge, so let me just say that it involved the use of native plants, powdered graphite, 10W-30 motor oil, and a roll of duct tape.) When we were done, I am not sure that the Man Upstairs Himself was able to detect us. We could hardly detect each other.

Victor Charlie led us at a half-run along a dry creek bed and around some rock outcroppings and through a grove of cinnamon trees.

"Hey! Cinnamon," Postlethwaite said. He stopped and stripped off some of the bark. **"We used to get cinnamon toast for Sunday brunch at Plimpton House at Yale** and then go in to chapel to hear Reverend Chubb. Good fellow. Terrific homilies. Brotherhood and all that." We tried to shush him, and then a Soviet-made 130-mm gun lobbed a few rounds our way **WHAMMA WHAMMA** and uprooted a tree near me. I dove

to avoid it and felt myself falling through an opening in the earth and sliding down a long slanting hole—a VC tunnel!

I slid on my belly, M-1 braced in front of me, and came to a sudden stop when that tunnel dead-ended at another. It was about six feet high and brightly lit by strings of tiny bulbs. I heard voices approach, the harsh metallic twang of Vietnamese, and I ducked into a recess cut into the red earth. Two VC in black pajamas passed within inches of my face, toting a radio antenna, and a third, a white rabbit, lugging a carton that said "Morrell Wieners." I thought, We just got here and already they're eating our lunch. The bare footsteps died away quickly and my ears picked up distant voices and the sound of running water—and the sound of rock 'n' roll. Evidently the VC had found Led Zeppelin's "Is It Hot Enough for You?"

> **Is it hot enough for you?**
> **Is it hot enough for you?**
> **Is your skin clammy enough?**
> **Is your heart pounding the way you like it?**
> **Have you wet your pants about as often as you hoped to?**
> **Have you shriveled far enough down in your shorts?**

And just then I felt a sharp tug at my sleeve. My left ventricle almost slammed shut.

It was Victor. "Too dangelous heel, you forrow," he whispered, and led me back up the exit ramp and into the jungle. "Many many tunners in hirr," he said. "We come back ratel." He set off at a trot and I followed. I believed that the other Walruses were right behind me but with our level of camouflage I couldn't be 100 percent sure.

We came over a hill and across a clearing, the grass up to our armpits, and suddenly there were ARVN choppers overhead and a big American Chinook hovering at about one thousand feet. Then Postlethwaite whipped off his shirt and stood and waved it in circles. The big dumbhead! I tackled him and threw him to the ground but it was too late. The ARVNs cut loose with everything they had. **RACKETA-RACKETA! WHUMP! WHUMP! WHOOSH!** Rockets, bullets, flares—the air whistled with projectiles.

I thought, This is one big free-fire zone and it's time for Big Boy to get out of it! I knew there was no such thing as medical evacuation for a Walrus. We were issued a double ration of gin and told where to place the barrel on our temple.

We made a dash for the tree line and Victor gestured toward a path about the width of a snake's waist and we Walruses bounded along it, following the tiny guy in black. I couldn't see anybody but I could hear them panting. I guess we must've run eighty or eighty-five miles.

I was galloping along through the jungle and then Victor stopped and I put on the brakes and Johannesen crashed into me and Cohen into him and O'Connell and Rodriguez and Jennings and Postlethwaite, and a few minutes later the CO arrived, still ashen-faced, glassy-eyed. "Rye down," Victor said.

We hit the ground and curled up, thinking we'd grab a few minutes of shut-eye. I was asleep the moment my head touched Mother Earth and briefly I was lying under a trailer at the Minnesota State Fair, my fingers touching Francine, and then I was awake, sitting bolt upright. Postlethwaite had gotten into his gin ration. He stood in the clearing singing "The Whiffenpoof Song" and when he got to the *Baa baa baa*, there was a tremendous **BOOM** and an orange fireball **FROOOSHH** and I turned and couldn't believe what I saw.

A Soviet-made T-54 tank rolling through the elephant grass, snapping off jungle trees like matchsticks, heading straight for us!

We dove for cover as it sprayed the area with hot lead, its turret gun roaming left to right, the steel face of the behemoth advancing like an implacable foe.

"That thar tank is about as welcome as a pig in the asparagus patch!" drawled Jennings.

You can get overconfident in a tank, though. You sit there at the controls feeling impregnable and forget there are Walruses in the world who know how to operate a can opener. I waited for the T-54 to roll abreast of me and

 stop and I set a charge in his treads and pressed the magic twanger and ducked and the tank rose as if on a hydraulic lift and when he came down he had the mobility of a dog turd. One moment a deadly tool of destruction and the next, a lawn ornament.

He must've radioed for support, though, because NVA

guns sent a few rounds whomping **BUMBA-BUMBA-BUMBA**
into the vicinity, testing, searching, and then a full barrage,
and suddenly the sky was full of Jap Zeros coming out of the
clouds, machine guns rattling like a can full of gravel, bullets zinging through the leaves! —A kamikaze squadron left
over from WW2, unable to accept the Emperor's defeat, had
kept their propeller craft in fighting trim at a secret jungle
airstrip waiting for the Wide Eyes to return! —The famous
Lost Squadron of the Rising Sun, four planes piloted by
men in their late seventies (who had, since the war, become
subsistence farmers and apostles of the late **Henry D. Thoreau**
and his philosophy of civil disobedience, that one man's
conscience is superior to the power of the state) and one by
one they dove at the Americans in the clearing, banging
away with their antique Gatlings. I dove behind the turret of
the T-54 and ripped a few bolts off the twisted blackened
track and then a Jap bomb struck the tank amidships and it
rose about ten feet up off the ground and I was left with no
cover, totally exposed, a sitting duck, the air full of black
smoke and the acrid smell of cordite and flames leaping
from the hatches and the VC driver in flames running
screaming and then Cohen came dashing toward me and
I yelled at him, "Abe! Down!" just as a Zero came screaming through the smoke and its twin cannon cut two parallel
furrows on either side of my buddy—and I just plain lost
my cool! —I went ballistic—I picked up a bolt and wound
up and hurled it with every ounce of hatred in my being

right smack through that Jap's windshield as he pulled out of his dive and I glimpsed his grinning face disappear in a cloud of busted glass as his plane went cartwheeling into the hill behind me and blew up.

And as suddenly as it had begun, it was all over.

The smoke blew away, the fire in the tank died out, and we Walruses wiped the camouflage away and sat down and tallied up the injuries: a few bruises, a pulled hamstring, a torn cartilage. Each of us carried thirty pounds of powdered nutrient in bags strapped across our chest and my nutrient had stopped fifteen bullets. I picked them out and tossed them away as the CO came up from the rear; he had recovered his faculties and was prepared to resume command. **"Walruses,** gather for debriefing," he snapped. We stood in loose formation, weapons at the ready.

He strode along the line, snapping a tiny riding crop against the palm of his hand, something I guess you learn at Annapolis. He stopped in front of Cohen. "Tell me what happened, trooper," he said, coolly. "From the very beginning."

"Okay," Cohen said. "I was born on December 13, 1950, in Sandusky, Ohio. My dad was the son of a rabbi. He operated a kosher dairy farm. His name was Isaac. My mom was a housewife. Her name was Naomi. I was the fourth child. The others were Sam, Susie, Reuben—we called him Scooter—"

"Okay, don't start from the beginning. Start with an hour ago."

We filled the CO in on the action and he wrote up his report.

"Walruses, at ease," he said, when all six copies had been separated and the carbons burned. "Prepare meal. Bed down at twenty hundred. Valente has the first watch, Cohen second, Rodriguez third. And Postlethwaite, I'm putting you in for a Medal of Honor for conspicuous bravery." Postlethwaite bowed his head, humbly. Jennings and I looked at each other and snickered. Victor returned with a helmet full of wild honey and an armload of bananas and yams, from which we made a sort of casserole, with cinnamon.

"The man on watch will also guard the prisoner," said the CO.

"He isn't a prisoner. He's a Walrus," I said. Victor grinned. He stripped off his black pajamas and we gave him a pair of drabs, the smallest we had, but Cohen had to take the pants in at the waist and in the rear. Victor preferred no cuffs, please, and no pleats in front, snug in the crotch, no drape. The shirt likewise was too broad in the shoulders and the cuffs hung down to his knees. But in a couple minutes, Cohen got him in good military order. He looked up at me proudly and said, "I am a Warrus now."

The Rodent

And that was how I met The Rodent. O'Connell nicknamed him, after his prominent nose and his long thin pigtail that resembled a rat's more than a pig's.

I shook his hand and barked the Walrus welcome. And all the others barked.

"You no carr me Victol no mole," he said. "That enemy name. I be Lodent now." We shook again and I gave him half my bedroll and we bunked down side by side in the grass and I slept like a baby.

That was my first twenty-four hours in Vietnam and as things turned out, it was pretty much a typical day. There was so much action, gunfire, confusion, horror, that one day pretty much segued into the next. The Rodent became an indispensable part of our Walrus team. I was the strategist, he was the tactician; I set the goals, he found the way to achieve them.

He and I became close, much closer than we intended perhaps.

One day in the DMZ on our way to **Vinh Linh Province** in a monsoon rain, we Walruses were chasing a North Vietnamese division out of **Quang Tri.** The entire **U.S. 11th Armored Cavalry** was on one side of them, and me and my eight guys on the other, and I was on the phone with some major general in a command chopper who kept asking what my strength was. I told him I could bench-press 300 pounds and that I doubted he weighed more than that.

That shut him up for a while.

We had to cut some wire to cross a hill called **Hill 249** through heavy overgrowth in a rubber plantation honeycombed with NVA tunnels and bunkers and infested with claymore mines, and suddenly we came under a fusillade from an ARVN firebase at **Luong Nghia Dung.** "Dung is the right name for them," I muttered, and I told The Rodent to get on the radio to tell the poopheads to hold fire, which he did.

Are you getting all of this down, by the way?

GHOST:
Of course. Everything.

You sure? You're not taking many notes.

GHOST:
The tape recorder is on.

What if it fails?

GHOST:
It won't, but if it did, I could reconstruct the whole thing.

I don't care to be reconstructed. Especially not by you.

GHOST:

The recorder light is on and the cassette is turning.

Yeah, well—your feet are on the floor, your eyes are open. That doesn't mean you're smart.

GHOST:

You want I should stop the tape and check it?

You get one little word wrong, one nuance misshaped, and it's war between you and me, you read?

GHOST:

I am doing the best I can.

You are not a writer, only a ghost. This is my story. We use my words. I don't want to find words like "pellucid" in here.

GHOST:

Check.

So the 11th was sending 155-mm howitzer shells up toward **Hill 249** where the NVA was dug in and then the pellucid sky blossomed with chutes—the **101st Airborne**—and pretty soon the **7th Cav** wanted in on the show and the **3rd Pag** and the **102nd Airborne** and **103rd** and air traffic controllers were going nuts trying to keep separation between the planes—our mission was to break the back of the Red siege of the Marines at Khe Sanh, but clearly some brass at HQ wanted to get their tickets punched, and at one point I lost it completely. I went totally ballistic.

THE PURR OF A MACHINE-GUN

I had just come around a bend in a creek bed and seen two VC mortar crews setting up their tubes and bipods and dashed in for some hand-to-hand, The Rodent on my heels, and together we hog-tied the ten of them and stacked them like cordwood and assembled the mortars and rained shells on 249 to set off those claymores so the 11th could sail in, machine guns purring, and blow up the tunnels and in the midst of our hellacious assault, just as we scored a bull's-eye on an NVA ammo dump and sent half the hill into the sky, the phone rang. I picked it up.

It was a colonel somewhere in Officeland who wondered who had authorized the mortar barrage.

I told him what I thought of him and his mother and I referred to his intelligence and character in the most unflattering terms. I used combinations of profanity that hadn't even been invented yet.

"You are an inflamed cyst on the butt of history," I said. "You can hide in the men's can of the **Joint Chiefs of Staff** and I will find you and pull your pants around your ankles and hang you from the stanchion like a pig in a butcher shop and you will squeal until they come and cut you down."

The Rodent listened with interest as I described in some

detail the torments I would inflict on the colonel's physiognomy. It takes a lot to make a colonel cry, and when I succeeded I hung up and threw the phone into a stagnant pool and The Rodent and I hiked into **Quang Tri City** and found, in the midst of the smoking ruins, a bar called **Juicy Lucy** and I showed the Laotian bartender how to make a hamburger correctly, very rare, cool in the middle, with a slice of raw onion and mustard, and a raw egg in a china cup and a shot of gin. The Rodent and I ate our fill and got drunk and told each other our life stories.

I told about Gladys and Arv and Eunice and Arvonne and Gorgeous George and the Baldies and how I was reincarnated through weight lifting and put aside my Cliffordness and became the Big Boy, and he told me about his boyhood on the rice plantation, his schooling at the *lycée* and later in Beijing, his training as a kick boxer and black-belt **tai dai** master, and to show me his mastery of the ancient martial art, he made himself disappear before my very eyes. I never saw anything like it.

A *tai dai* maneuver called Plucking the Orchid

I looked at the bartender and he looked at me. We waited. A fork moved. A spoon was bent. A glass fell to the floor. And then the **pepper shaker** rose from the table and overturned and there was a tremendous sneeze and The Rodent appeared.

That was how he reentered the physical realm, through "the doorway of a sneeze," he explained.

The secret of his disappearance he would not reveal. He had taken an oath.

He did, however, demonstrate an exercise called **"Plucking the Orchid,"** in which you draw your opponent's strength away from him and use it to throw him on his keester.

1. Stand with your weight evenly balanced on both feet, your back relaxed, head erect, arms at sides.
2. Step forward onto left foot and extend arms forward toward opponent.
3. Visualize him as a small piece of vegetation.
4. Hurl him to the ground and step back and take a deep breath.

It was, he said, **the key to domination** of any situation. He promised someday he would teach me how to disappear.

One night, at Kilometer 75 on Route 9 on our way into Laos, in an ancient ceremony that involved opening veins and exchanging blood and peeing into a single pot and offering each other a snot sandwich, we became brothers. "Now you and me, we as crose as two nomer men can be," he said, chewing. We stuck together like glue, the 250-pound Walrus and his 87-pound pup, we fought side by side and when **Mom Oxnard** sent me big packages full of goodies, I shared them with him and he developed a taste for Swedish *lefse* and watermelon pickles and raspberry jam and Velveeta and Ritz crackers. ("Litz clackas," to him.) We went on leave together and made the rounds of the **gin mills of Saigon** and inspected the crowds of women standing on the curb, women in green dresses the color of a neon sign over a door

that door and he saved my life more than once.

In Hue I was with a bar girl named Ngo Ngu Gai Ngao who
had a bosom you could stack cups and saucers on and she
was fixing me a gin rickey in her apartment above the **Perfume River Saloon.** She said, "Jimmy, you have a beautiful soul.
I have been in your company for only three hours and yet I
feel we are **spiritual twins,** you and me," and she bent to remove her shoes and **I saw London, I saw France,** and then The Rodent raced in from the balcony and he shoved me out the
door and a moment later the couch I had been sitting on was
riddled with a hundred rounds from an automatic rifle she
kept stashed in her closet. To me it had looked like an ironing board. I had thought she was going to do my pants. Instead, she tried to do me.

Afterward, he and I went to a bar and started tossing back
whiskey sours and got drunk together, and it was then I
realized what a ferocious spirit lay inside this little guy.

He insisted on sticking with me, drink for drink, though
he was one third my body weight.

I tried to explain this to him that night, and though he
was lying under the table, he sprang up and grabbed a knife
and put it to my throat.

"Aporogize, Big Boy," he snarled. "You say Lodent cannot hord his riquor? That is farse! Farse!"

I apologized, but I saw a scary side of The Rodent right
then that would come back to haunt me. On the surface, he

was semi-American and could talk pro football or fishing lures or auto mechanics and laugh and kid around and be regular, but underneath was a trip wire that triggered something crazed and obsessive in his nature.

CHAPTER 9

JIMMY RETURNS STATESIDE

My tour of duty in Nam ended on Thanksgiving Day 1970. I was tempted to stay, but by then the war was lost, what with all the campus demonstrations that tied the hands of the President and denied the tools of victory to the American fighting man, so I didn't bother to re-up.

One night when we pulled patrol duty along the Ho Chi Minh Trail, a Walrus named Walt Unruh told me all about his home along the **Iditarod Trail** in Alaska and how you could take off in your float plane from **Anchorage** and in twenty minutes land on a sky-blue wilderness lake with no living soul within thirty miles and toss your lure in the water and catch a **king salmon.**

The Rodent wasn't with me then. He was furious at me because, weeks before, he had offered me a cup of hot sake and I said, kidding, "What is this? a children's drink? Somebody put syrup in it?" He got sore and said he never wanted to speak to me again.

So there I was with Walt, sitting in a tree stand a hundred feet above the ground, watching for NVA, drinking **Four**

Roses, leg-wrestling to see if we could throw each other off the platform, and then he challenged me to a peeing contest. We each peed straight up over our heads and mine went four feet higher up the tree than his.

"It's all in the wrists," I said.

"The North is man's country," he said. "Up there, you can write your name in the snow nine months out of the year. The world is your urinal. Women are compliant, being outnumbered six to one. Nobody cares if you bathe or not or whether you eat with your fingers or lean to one side in your chair and let her rip. And cold weather, you know, is a proven aphrodisiac. Northern men can go all night where southern guys peter out in fifteen minutes."

Sitting in a tree in Vietnam, I thought Alaska sounded wonderful. After two years of jungle life, frozen tundras seemed like a piece of cake.

The day I left Vietnam, Gladys wrote to me: "Clifford, your status as a veteran will give you preference in civil service hiring. Did you know that? You can get into the **postal service** and enjoy lifetime security."

But I did not care about preference. I wanted Lady Luck to look at me and grin and bestow **vast unimaginable favors.** I wanted a big life, not one spent looking at small rectangular compartments.

I flew Da Nang to Los Angeles first class aboard a North-west Orient 747. The night before, I had jumped out of that tree, my face painted, with a shirtful of hand grenades, and stopped an NVA tank unit, me and Walt together, hurling the deadly missiles into a maelstrom of fire and smoke as chunks of steel flew past our heads and NVA regulars massed for a counterattack, and twelve hours later I plopped down in a wide seat and a tall blonde from Oshkosh asked if I'd like a drink before take-off. She had a bone structure a guy could spend a whole afternoon getting to know better.

"I'd like a glass of gin and a raw egg in a china cup," I said. "And later, a hamburger, rare, with a raw onion." She asked if I wanted the gin with Mountain Dew or 7-Up.

"Excuse me, ma'am, but that would be like putting rhinestones on the Mona Lisa," I said.

I imagined Arnold and me becoming pals and going off and doing stuff together.

I was given the seat for meritorious service by the CO whose butt I'd saved from certain court-martial when I told the higher-ups that he was leading the unit in battle on a particular day he had chosen to spend at the beach at Qui Nhon with a honey named **Dixie Dexter.**

"Where were you stationed?" the blonde purred when she set down my drink.

I figured she had got her fill of heroic tales from all the desk officers and wouldn't be impressed by my activities,

so I told her I had spent two years in the Quartermaster Corps assembling bunk beds.

"That must have been interesting," she said.

In L.A., mustered out of the Walruses, I hung around hoping to meet my hero **Arnold Schwarzenegger,** whom I had met briefly in **Cam Ranh** where he was entertaining the troops with feats of muscular display, posing in his **leopardskin briefs.** He had autographed my helmet and told me to look him up Stateside. So I did. I somehow imagined Arnold and me becoming close pals and going off on trips to remote places and doing stuff together, fishing, camping, canoeing, horseback riding. I hung around the lobby of **Pectoral Pictures** for most of two afternoons and drank dozens of cherry Cokes, no sign of Arnold, and the brunette receptionist was getting more and more tight-lipped about when he might put in an appearance.

"He's very busy right now," was all she'd say. "He's involved in a number of projects."

"I am involved in some projects myself, and one of them is my mission to meet **Arnold** again and renew our friendship from Vietnam," I told her. "I am a Walrus. You may not be aware of that. I happen to know that Arnold is thinking about making a picture about the Walruses."

"I will tell him you were here," she said, and she went back to her typing, which did not appear to be her strong suit.

So I left him a note:

Dear Hero, I came, I waited, I drank cherry Cokes, I left. My feelings about you are unchanged. You are **John Wayne**'s rightful successor and will surely become the greatest actor and filmmaker in America. We met at the **U.S. Navy base at Cam Ranh Bay** last fall when you graciously came to entertain our troops and I shared with you my dream of someday assisting you in your career of making great motion pictures that capture the human spirit. I am sure we will meet again. Meantime, know that you are the greatest and that the American fighting man is 100% on your side.

Jimmy (Big Boy) Valente

I went to a nearby diner and ate a hamburger, rare, with raw onion. I had about five grand in back pay and an airline pass to anywhere in the U.S. It was time to move on and I chose **Fairbanks.** It was time to close the book on **Clifford Oxnard** and let the Jimmy in me learn to fly.

CHAPTER 10

JIMMY HEADS NORTH

I called Gladys from the airport and told her I'd been assigned to the far North, a hush-hush assignment involving our nation's **NORAD defenses.**

"I baked a pie for you," she said, softly. "I'm fixing you a

meat loaf. I've got your room all cleaned. I bought new curtains. A new TV."

I told her I was sorry but I had to put America first.

"Oh, Clifford," she said. "My heart has been broken so many times you can hear it jingle when I walk. First, Arv runs off with the hygienist and then Arvonne marries a saxophonist who treats her like furniture and now Eunice decides she is Lebanese. She's a professor at the University with pierced nipples and no prospect of marriage and family, and now you go running off to Alaska. Why?"

"I have to sing my song and dance my dance, Mom," I said.

She said that **Grandma Oxnard** had died and gone to **heaven,** and that she, Gladys, was hoping for something similar. "I am so sick of fixing meat loaf I could spit," she said bitterly. "The smell of tuna casserole makes me gag."

I advised her to sell the **House of Lunch** and move to a luxury apartment with a balcony and a washer-dryer and not tell Eunice where she had gone.

"I pray for you every day," she said. "I pray that you come home and take the civil service exam and become a city fireman or a postal worker and make your mama proud of you."

Instead I went into professional wrestling.

It happened like this.

I landed in **Fairbanks** on Christmas Eve. The airport wind sock stuck straight out, pointing east. Snowbanks as big as

New Hampshire. The landscape looked as if it had never known life in any form, animal or vegetable. I rented a back room in a house trailer on the edge of town, an old trailer surrounded by junked cars and oil barrels, with a satellite dish out back and a BEWARE OF OWNER sign in front. He was a guy named White Blaze who resided in the front room and earned his living with a deck of cards. He had been a thoracic surgeon in Memphis and got addicted to muscle relaxants which did him no good in surgery but helped his poker playing enormously and after he had perfected his game (losing a wife and two homes in the process), he emigrated north, to where money flowed freely, where the sun rose at eleven and set at one and there was little else to do with money except risk it in manly games of chance, and he parlayed a small nest egg into a quarter-million dollars one afternoon in the back room of **Ike's Pool Hall,** in a game of **Roll Em** with a couple truckdrivers and a mysterious figure named Duke, who sat peeling the thousands off his roll and never came near the bottom. He told me all this as we sat eating egg rolls and watching a **Dick Powell** detective movie. He had peroxided his hair and dyed a blue streak up the middle. He wore a black silk shirt and smoked black Russian cigarettes, his manicured nails were painted pink and sprinkled with sparkle dust, he had a gold tooth tipped with a diamond and rhinestone earrings in the shape of a W and a B. "A person's gotta have a look, kid," he said. "It takes people's minds off their cards."

Everybody I met in Fairbanks was someone who'd screwed up big-time in the Lower Forty-Eight. Gratuitous screwups. You drank with them, shot pool with them, and

eventually the story leaked out, how they'd come from good families and were given all the advantages and then started vandalizing cemeteries or fooling around with a sister-in-law or got hooked on cough medicines, maybe embezzled from the March of Dimes or swiped the Hopi tapestry from the sanctuary of the Unitarian church (and then tried to sell it to the Methodists) or tried to shoplift a garden tractor or assaulted an elderly crossing guard or how one day, out of pure boredom, they started phoning in bomb threats to nursing homes. Having thus hit bottom and become social pariahs, they hitch-hiked to **Fairbanks** to remake their lives as short-order cooks and reside in a trailer in a climate where, for half the year, you don't need a freezer.

"I come from an old Memphis family, a family of doctors and lawyers and literary men, and my father was an Episcopalian prelate," **White Blaze** told me, "and I trotted off to **Vanderbilt** and married a fine woman and lived in a big white mansion with all the trimmings and begat four fine children, and yet I knew it was only a matter of time before I threw it away. I waited for degradation to happen and it was a big relief when it did. I tried alcohol and then adultery and then larceny and finally it was those muscle relaxants that did the trick."

I didn't hope to emulate him, but my five grand leaked away in about a month, half of it spent on a **used Rambler** that wouldn't ramble, and I was forced to hike into town and find work. At first I thought I'd like to get my trucker's license and wrestle eighteen-wheelers up the **Alcan Highway** for a few years, but the AAA Acme A-1 Alaska Trucker School couldn't take me until September, eight months away, so I went to the courthouse and took a civil service exam and got into **the post office,** sorting parcel post.

I lasted half a day.

I learned something fundamental about myself that morning. Jimmy (Big Boy) Valente is not happy in a confined space performing tasks assigned to him by small-minded people. The art of clerical sorting does not engage my mind: **the cogs simply do not mesh.** I need not say more. I stuck to my post until lunch hour and then looked around at the cubicle, the helpful lists and charts taped to the wall, the pigeonholes, the tape and scissors and ruler and paper clips, and I said good-bye to it **as a bear would say good-bye to a leg trap** and went out to lunch and stayed there.

I went into **Mom's Cafe** next to Ike's and **George Jones** was singing "Another Man in My Bed, Another January in Duluth."

> **It's been a hard winter, and my mind is about to crack**
> **I'm sitting in the dark with a mountain of beer cans out back.**
> **White snow, black trees, gray sky—for Christmas she told me**
> **   good-bye,**
> **But it's nice in Duluth and it's bound to warm up in July.**

I ordered a hamburger, very rare, with a raw onion, mustard, a glass of gin, and a raw egg yolk in a china cup. And when I swallowed the yolk and chased it with gin, I looked in the bottom of the china cup and there, taped to it, was **a red rose.** And a note.

It said, "You blothel who you abandoned in Vietnam without one word of expranation is standing behind you with a Cort .38 behind you light ear and he not happy."

I turned in slow motion and looked down the gun barrel to The Rodent's arm and him at the end of it, a faint smile on his thin lips.

I stood up slowly and slowly assumed the posture of **"Plucking the Orchid."** Weight evenly balanced, back relaxed, head erect, arms at sides. And I barked the **Walrus** phrase for "You and I, forever."

He smiled. "We speak the same ranguage," he said. He put the gun in his belt and shook my hand. "You rook good."

I was wearing black jeans (32-inch waist), a black shirt with pearl buttons (58-inch chest), snakeskin cowboy boots, and a polar-bear parka and was looking good but feeling rotten, being broke and without a prospect in the world. He seemed to sense that.

He was wrestling, he told me, for the I.W.W., International World Wrestling, which was eight wrestlers and a promoter named **Felix,** staging matches from the Yukon to the North Slope of Alaska. He was matched against another bantamweight named **Billy the Boy Bully** and earned one hundred dollars per match and six or seven times that in side bets and was wrestling two and sometimes three matches a day.

"Lessring vely vely good to Victol Charry," he said.

He showed me a poster for an I.W.W. show, with a picture of him scowling, in black pajamas **("Victor Charlie the Terror of the DMZ")**, and pictures of some other monsters, none of whom scared me in the slightest.

CHAPTER 11
THE I.W.W.

I found Felix the next day in Mom's, spooning his moose noodle soup. He was a hatchet-faced little weasel whose narrow head supported a toupee that looked like a raccoon crushed under a semi, all eighteen wheels. He had glazed it with gel and it glittered like cat turds in the moonlight. He wore a particularly livid green plaid sport coat made of petrochemicals, a sportcoat you wanted to shoot and put out of its misery, and a yellowish shirt and blue-blob tie and brown slacks with a lived-in look. He was the unhealthiest-looking human being I had ever laid eyes on, very sallow and liverish-looking, all splotches and rheum and exploded capillaries, a stub of a cigarette smoldering on his lower lip, a fresh one on its way. He lit it and cast his bulbous eyes on me and said, "Victor mentioned you to me, kid. Glad to meetcha." And he reached into his breast pocket, smoke curling up around his chops, and pulled out a roll of cash big enough to choke a hippo and peeled off fifteen hundreds and handed them over. "That's for fifteen minutes of your time. Siddown, kid."

So I sat and listened.

Felix as host of "The Big Bandstand"

"I usedta be in radio. Felix Dorbal, **'The Big Bandstand.'** Coast-to-coast in the Forties, and in 1954 I was coast-to-toast. Elvis killed popular music. Suddenly it wasn't popular anymore. So I switched to sports. I'm a guy whose idea of exercise is opening a beer bottle with a twist-off cap but I could see where the money is. I managed the **Barberan** barnstorming baseball team for a summer, ran some bowling tournaments, managed the billiards champ **Studs (The Judge) Tony** for a year, then I met a wrestler named **Wes Bitman.** He was stranded in St. Paul and trying to sell his car for gas money to get home to Milwaukee. I made him into Rasputin the Mad Russian. Long hair, beard, black satin cape, and he glowered a lot. It was 1958. In six months he was hot in Minnesota, Milwaukee, St. Louis, and then he got on TV and he was hot everywhere at once. We flew in our private DC-3, crisscrossed the country. **He was big for ten years** and got fat and happy and retired to his avocado ranch in **Fresno.** So I came here to start up a new pro wrestling circuit, International World Wrestling. Alaska is temporary. I'm aiming for Vegas. Friend of mine manages the **Diamond Dunes.** We've got a terrific show here. Eight guys. You fight the

same guy every day, you get to know each other's moves, it's like ballet. Good money. Winter is great. No sun for three months, and the towns full of construction guys and oil workers, their pockets full of dough, going stir-crazy, desperate for entertainment, and these are not theatergoers here. Not a big market for Renaissance music. The night shift gets off at seven in the morning and by seven forty-five they're pretty well oiled and that's when we put on our first show. We'll pack a hangar, a warehouse, with two or three thousand men, all of them betting like mad—I'll handle your side action for you—and when we've milked that cow, we go up the road to the next venue and do it again at four and come back to the first place for the midnight show. You go out and perform and I handle all the monkey business. How does four hundred a day sound?"

It sounded good to me. Better than what I'd ever earn driving a truck. It sounded fantastic. I packed my stuff and Felix's bus picked me up at noon. An old Eskimo guy named **Iron Eyes** was at the wheel and Felix was camped in the seat behind him, wrapping bundles of tens and twenties and plopping them in an open suitcase. It was almost full. Behind him, sprawled across the seats, leaning every which way, buried under quilts and bear skins were eight men fast asleep, mouths agape, each one snoring in a different tempo and key, each one quietly emitting his own brand of gas. One man, who had a dirty blond beard, wore a horned helmet and a sleep mask. The floor was littered with pista-

chio shells and empty beer cans and crusts of sandwiches. The aroma was pretty stiff and a guy would think twice about lighting a match: between the alcohol and the methane, the bus had enough fuel to achieve low orbit.

Felix nodded toward the helmeted man. "That's Svend. He's the foreman. Soon as he wakes up, he'll work you into the show."

I flopped down in back and a crusty old dude in the seat opposite opened one bloodshot eye and said, "You wouldn't be interested in purchasing a crossbow and a broadsword and a Satan cape, would you? Sell you the whole kit and caboodle and toss in my Mongolian goatskin boots free, all for five hundred bucks. What do you say?"

I said it sounded good but what would I use them for?

"I'll toss in a wooden altar, six candles, a hex medallion, and a vial of powdered elk antler," he said.

He reached over and shook my hand. "I'm the Duke of Dubuque and this sad sack next to me is the Dauphin Louie de Louie." He nodded toward a figure wrapped in a horse blanket, dead to the world, snoring like a Piper Cub on takeoff. The Duke leaned toward me, confidentially. **"We are only temporarily in the wrestling line while we get our real-estate licenses.** Came to Alaska last spring with **a theater troupe.** Did Beckett and Shepard and all the newer playwrights. Did some improv too, of course. Taught acting, stage movement, public speaking, dance, deconstruction if there was a call for it. But alas, **Alaska is no fit home for the artistic temperament.** The conceptual way of thinking is not welcome in the North, my boy. These are engineers, not savants. **And so we were forced to join this gang of cretins and thugs and common ruffians."**

He lowered his voice. "I blush to say it, but the Dauphin and I wrestle in the altogether. **Au naturel, in other words.** It's been a big hit and a boon to our social lives, but it's time to move on."

He leaned closer. "I sense that you possess a noble spirit, sir, and that I can confide in you." He glanced at the Dauphin to make sure he was truly asleep. "I am the illegitimate son of **Nelson D. Rockefeller,"** he whispered. "A love child by an actress who shall remain nameless. Shoveled into an orphanage and deprived of my heritage so as not to compromise my father's presidential hopes. **A Rockefeller by birth,** entitled to a country estate and a fourteen-room apartment on **Sutton Place,** but instead—this." And he gestured limply toward the detritus in the bus aisle and dabbed at his eyes. **"A life of squalor in the frozen north among rug-chewing goons."**

I said, "You seem a little old to be the son of **Nelson Rockefeller."** The moment I said it, I could see I had struck a nerve.

The Duke looked away, stung, and said quietly, "I knew I shouldn't have put my trust in you. You're like all the others. Forgive me for imparting that information. And now excuse me. I must rest."

I tried to apologize but he waved it off. "It's nothing. A man's story is his own and he should keep it to himself. Silly of me to forget. Have a good life, sir."

I reached into my pocket and counted out three hundred dollars and that improved his disposition. "You won't regret this," he said. "Everything is of the best materials, believe me. **My byword is quality."**

CHAPTER 12

JIMMY THE FLOWER CHILD

I was going to ask the Duke why he was selling his cherished props and costumes, but then the bus turned at the **Fairbanks International Airport** sign and stopped in front of the **Paydirt Airline** terminal and the Duke shook his partner's shoulder. "Daylight in the swamps, your highness. Up and at 'em," he growled, and he hauled down a duffel bag from the overhead and shouldered it and marched off the bus, the **Dauphin** slinking behind. Felix gave them each a manila envelope and shook hands and into the terminal they went.

I asked Felix later if the Duke had left me a cape and spear and he said, "Everything that old thief owned was in that duffel bag. If he had a spear, it must've been a miniature."

While I was digesting that particular bit of information, Felix patted the seat next to him. I sat down.

"Big Boy, I have come to a decision. The show needs a fairy, and, son, you're the one who can do it for us."

"Someone just cut a big one in here," I said. "My, my, that is a cheese that died a long time ago." Felix said he

didn't smell anything. "It's always the culprit who can't smell it," I replied.

He said, "Your name will be The Flower Child, and you'll come out and mince around with daffodils twined about your brow and a peace sign painted on your scalp and you'll blow kisses to the crowd and talk about the importance of preserving the environment and not doing anything to negatively impact the caribou herds."

"Please. No. I am a Navy veteran." I begged him. "People will shun me in the street, nobody will sit next to me in bars, even hookers will look at me with moral disfavor."

"Exactly. And we'll double the gate, kid. **We need that extra attraction.** We got all the heroes we can stand, what we need is somebody the crowd can hate. There's nothing that brings joy to so many people like giving them the chance to despise you."

"I'd rather kill myself with a dull knife."

"Please. For the guys' sake. For the sake of the pure art of wrestling."

"What would my Walrus buddies think if they saw me? You can't make me do it, Felix."

He sighed. "This is a privilege, kid, what I'm offering you. Any idiot can be a hero. It takes ability to play a heel. Did you ever hear of acting? You think actors would rather play **George Washington** or **Count Dracula**? How about I pay you four hundred a match plus a slight percentage of the gate to maintain your interest?"

He was a persuasive guy, Felix. He appealed to my vanity. He made me feel like **Lon Chaney, Jr.** And that night I walked into the Tanana High School gymnasium with daffodils on my head and wearing beads and sandals and an R. Crumb T-shirt as Felix screamed, "At two hundred and thirty-eight pounds, in the tie-dye trunks, a man who wishes to dedicate this next match to his friends **Ralph Nader** and **Jane Fonda**—from Berkeley, California, The Flower Child!" and three thousand oil workers booed from the depths of their **beer-soaked hearts.**

I danced up the steps to the ring and posed for the crowd and grabbed the microphone and asked everyone to join me in singing "Give Peace a Chance" and someone yelled, "Give me a chance to get a piece of you, fruitcake!" and I ranted about love and brotherhood and about how the **exploitation of our precious oil resources** was interfering with **the breeding patterns of the great snowy owl** and that for the sake of our children we should place a moratorium on drilling until we learned how to lessen its impact on these owls and also on the **extremely rare snow spider** and the Arctic moth—I yik-yakked until everyone was standing and screeching and shaking their fists at me and frothing at the mouth, and my gosh what a thrill it was to have that audience in the palm of my hand—to stand in the ring and throw a pose and feel the anger flow your way—and then Yukon Bob came trotting down the aisle to thunderous acclaim, a figure of **manly rectitude** preceded by his booming belly, and he grinned a purposeful grin and heaved his great carcass into the ring and **bared his chest** and flexed his breasts and did a couple knee bends and we dove into a clinch and circled and I proceeded to whale away on him for a while, getting him in an illegal nostril-hold, rubbing his eyes along the top rope, giving him an instep stomp, a nipple pinch, playing my dirty tricks as the referee **Iron Eyes** looked on solemnly, until Bob was dizzy with pain and then came the heinous Hangman maneuver—hurling him into the ropes so his head caught between them and he flipped over and hung by his neck and I kicked him a few times in the groin—Oh my! the pain! the exquisite suffering!—and then came the Backbreaker and then somehow Bob struggled free of my grasp. **He shook his noble head.** His nostrils flared. His outrage was awakened. He popped me one on the jaw and I fell and convulsed for a while and the crowd was in ecstasy. He whaled away on me and I popped my blood cartridges and the audience ate from our hands, it was exactly what three thousand sex-starved pipe fitters sky-high on boilermakers wanted to see at twilight on a Wednesday in December, blood smeared on the canvas, and The Flower Child in a dazed stupor, poleaxed by Yukon Bob's *Flying Augur*, and the victor modestly acknowledging the cheers and **the vile environmentalist,** bloody and dejected, hustled away by security guys warding off the drunks trying to kick me in the gonads, and then Bob and me had a beer, showered, climbed on the bus, and Felix said that the gate was twice what he'd estimated and Yukon and Mike and Dave and Felix continued their bridge game as we rolled on toward **Koyukuk** and me and The Rodent sat in back and reminisced about our Walrus days.

"Those Walrus days wirr nevel come again," he said. "Rike sprendol in the glass, rike groly in the frowel."

"Speak for yourself, Commie," I retorted. "Big Boy here is doing just fine." I had earned fifteen hundred bucks that first day, what with the percentage of gate. I counted it six times. My gosh, it was like a license to steal. To ride around on a bus and sleep and three times a day go and work hard for fifteen minutes—who couldn't handle that?

The I.W.W. routine was a snap compared to Vietnam. We wrestled three bouts a day, six days a week, and ate four meals a day, and slept two to a bed. I bunked with The Rodent who thrashed in his sleep but perhaps I did too. The chow was good if you like baloney sandwiches. We passed through **Fairbanks** every week to pick up our laundry from **Talkeetna Drip Dry** where an Inuit woman starched everything so the seam of your undershorts was like a Bowie knife. You had to soak the starch out. We worked six days a week, and on Monday, our day off, we chowed down on unabridged T-bone steaks washed down with a snootful of hooch strong enough to take the chrome off a **Cadillac.** We continued drinking at a nightclub where ugly women dance on your table and you stuff twenties in their garter belts and they remove their underwear. One night we went to an outdoor theater to see a Tarzan movie starring **Johnny Weissmuller.** Thirty below and the concession stand sold you a bag of whale blubber and the picture was projected against the side of a glacier,

Tarzan, his great naked chest glittering as he swung through the trees. We sat in the snow and drank and awoke at 5 A.M. with headaches you could split kindling with and crawled out of bed and resumed the suffering.

We wrestled in hangars, warehouses, the holds of ships, we wrestled in mud, or coated with oil, and sometimes we wrestled in a ring with a few thousand live mackerel flopping around, just for the added interest. The alpha wrestler was **Svend the Yellow-Toothed,** a Nordic warrior with shoulder-length snowy blond hair and a caribou-skin cape with the head and teeth intact, and there was **Ahmad Jihad**

Svend the Yellow-Toothed

in Bedouin robes and **Oberkapitan Werner Wehrmacht** with his black boots and jodhpurs and gleaming monocle, and **Ivan the Terrible** in his fur cap and red sickle-and-hammer cape, and there was **Victor Charlie** the 87-pound terrorist racing around the ring snarling and spitting at **Little Billy.** There were various heroes, **Yukon Bob** and **Matanuska Mike** and **Dawson Dave.** And there was me, the utility man. I was The Flower Child and then became Dr. Death for a while and then Wotan and for matinees the Creature from Krakatoa.

Svend had the best rant of anybody. He'd grab the microphone away from Felix, the ring announcer, and yell that he had been wrestling professionally for fifteen years and yet never, **never in his career,** had he ever set foot in the ring with such heinous trash as this—and he pointed at his opponent,

whoever it was—and he cried out, "I put it to you, the fans: What shall I do with this bucket of pus, this pisspot, this slab of maggots, this execrable atrocity against nature, this pile of abominations?"

And the crowd roared, **"KILL HIM!"**

And Svend the Yellow-Toothed asked the fans on the opposite side of the arena, and they felt that homicide was the only fair solution, too.

Svend climbed up onto the turnbuckle and screamed, "I will thrash him, lash him, paste him, waste him, batter and lambaste him, and force the contemptuous blackguard to crawl across the ring and lick the sweat off my socks!"

This suited the crowd just fine.

Sometimes his opponent was Ivan, the perfidious Russian, and sometimes it was Prince Harry Belial, and sometimes it was me.

"Behold this degenerate molester of women!" he screeched, pointing at me one night when I was taking a night off from The Flower Child and wrestling under the name Richard Speck. "A despoiler of innocent girls, a runaway from justice—well, tonight, my friends, this putrid pervert gets the punishment he deserves!" And the crowd roared, like high surf hitting a cliff, and Svend hurled himself at me and we locked arms and he said, "Stomp and chin kick," and I stomped on his foot, and he fell down, writhing, and I took a run at him and kicked him about two inches east of his chin, and he clutched at his face and toppled over and lay, legs twitching, and I dove on him for the pin and he said, "Fourteen, double T, seventy-eight, sixteen," and I jumped up and climbed onto the turnbuckle and jumped, my feet landing a couple inches south of his testicles, and he flopped over and writhed around on his belly as if he'd been reamed with a hot poker, and I got him in a toe twist, and that caused him no end of agony—of course the audience by now was foaming and raging freely, standing on their chairs, trying to hurl beer at me—and then I smacked him in the small of his back, and he screamed and banged his forehead on the canvas and his legs twitched, and then I got him in the Stretcher hold, and he was in hellish agony, but not so much that he couldn't tell me what came next— "Forty-four, nineteen, thirty-six, ten, and down double," he said, and then he managed to wriggle out of the Stretcher, bonk me on the forehead, run and carom off the ropes and do a flying mule and knock me down, do a pile driver, get me in a half nelson, and pin me, and leap up, arms raised, for the adulation of the mob, as I slithered under the ropes and into the protective custody of the ushers and limped back to the dressing room, properly chastened.

And afterward Svend and I would have a beer and he gave me pointers on how to improve my performance, how to roar better and harangue the crowd and work on my rant, using a thesaurus to piece together new expressions, like "malodorous moron" and "nefarious nincompoop" and "perfidious pipsqueak."

He explained how to receive his flying mule and flop throat-first against the top rope and hang there by my chin, tongue out, eyes crossed, to be hauled off and put in a toehold and pinned. He taught me to get the right kind of trunks, with strong elastic waistbands so they stretch tight over your butt and don't bunch up in your crack. And a nut

Me as The Flower Child. Guys in Alaska hyperventilated at the sight.

cup that can stand up to a steel-toed boot or a folding chair. He taught me breathology and escapology and how, if you need to pee real bad during a bout, you have your opponent lift you up and do the Helicopter and the pee doesn't land in the ring.

I enjoyed being The Flower Child because I was good at it. I added a pink boa to the act and let my hair grow out long and dyed it blond and took to wearing long dangly earrings. The sight of earrings on a man in Alaska in the early seventies was enough to make a crowd go bananas. I loved being the bad dog who other dogs come around to sniff your butt and you sniff theirs and bite it as hard as you can.

I enjoyed being mischievous so much I started to tease The Rodent, forgetting that he was oriental and couldn't take a joke.

CHAPTER 13

THE DEADLY FEUD

One night as The Rodent slept, I filled up his pajama bottoms with butterscotch pudding. He threatened to kill me. So, to make peace, I gave him a cigar. He lit it and it exploded. He almost impaled himself on a doorknob trying to get the thing out of his mouth. The next night I took the lightbulb out of the socket in the dressing room can and put Saran Wrap over the toilet so when The Rodent peed, it all ran down on his shoe.

He came raging out, his shoes soaked, and all the guys fell over laughing, and he screamed, "One day I wirr clush you rike a pop can, Big Boy! I wirr lip your face off!" I laughed and tried to pat him on the head. He bit me, hard, on the wrist.

Felix told me to make peace with him. **"Don't go to war with Asians; once engaged, they never relent or forget,"** he said.

So I offered The Rodent a dozen longstemmed roses. He accepted them with elaborate thanks, said he had been a fool to get upset, to please forgive him, he would be my pal from now on, et cetera and so forth.

He started bringing me breakfast in bed. A little **tap tap tap** at the door at noon and in tiptoed the tiny gladiator, tray in hand, a glass of fresh-squeezed orange juice and a stack of buttermilk cakes and a dozen sausages and three bagels. My suspicions should have been aroused, but I am a Minnesotan, a trusting soul. He was, as it turned out, putting a mysterious homeopathic powder in the OJ that gave me the worse case of hemorrhoids in the Arctic, a set of butt grapes that made T-bone steaks not the pure pleasure they should have been. It got so I couldn't sit down. I had a foam dough-nut sewn into the seat of my trunks, which got me the nick-name Balloon Butt. And one night The Rodent spooned a jalapeño sauce called **Tijuana Cat Whiz** onto my T-bone that burned like blazes on the way out and also a soy supplement that resulted in a rock-hard stool. It was like passing an axe. I fainted in the can.

That was the night The Flower Child lost it. **I truly went ballistic.**

I was the last event, fighting Yukon Bob, and I hurt like blazes. I grabbed the mike and I bent over and pointed to the relevant spot and told the crowd to pucker up. I was out of my mind with pain. I told the crowd to stick their hands in their pants and see if they could find their manhood. I said I was proud to be an atheist and Communist and that I could beat anybody in the place with one hand. And then Bob came waltzing in and I tore him apart—he kept yelling in my ear, **"Cut it out, man! Slow down! What's got into you?"** and I kept whopping him in the chops, and the crowd went berserk and stormed the ring, waving two-by-fours and ball-peen hammers. **Iron Eyes** tore off his referee shirt and dove for safety, and **Yukon Bob** followed him, and I was all alone, surrounded by six thousand berserk oil riggers who were feeling no pain whatsoever.

I climbed up on the turnbuckle and held my arms up for silence and said, "Whoever wants to die first, step forward. I'll kill ten of you before you so much as scratch me, and probably by that time the cops will be here. And when I'm on trial for mass murder, I am going to plead diminished mental capacity on account of hemorrhoids, and believe me, in my case it's the truth. I am no flower child. I am a mad dog veteran of the U.S. Navy Walruses, a walking time bomb, my mind permanently warped by **Agent Orange,** and I want to die and take you with me!"

We never forget each other and that's why I'm proud to say "I am a Walrus!"

And two guys stepped forward with pistols drawn and knives in their teeth. The crowd shrank back.

"Walrus," they said. "Bark."

I barked the Walrus code for "brother."

They said, "You were kidding about the Communist stuff, right?" I barked in the affirmative.

They barked back, "Three Walruses together can rule any mob."

And we moved toward the now-silent crowd and they

melted away in front of us. We charged up the aisle and into the locker room and I pulled on my clothes while they guarded the bus against tire slashers and I ran to climb aboard and we three gave each other the Walrus neck lock and the secret woof and the snuffle of brotherhood. And then I walked to the back of the bus where The Rodent sat in the dark, his eyes glittering.

"I have taken enough crap from you, evil one," I said in a low cold voice. "It is enough to endure the bus rides, the darkness and cold, the drunken mobs, the lice-ridden hotels, the vile foods and condiments. I will no longer endure your **perfidious schemes** and **evil powders.**"

At that, he hissed and let out a squeal of rage and leaped for my throat and I felt a burning pain in my adam's apple where his sharp little incisors clamped on tight—it took Bob and Mike and Dave and Svend to pry him off me. He bit right through my turtleneck collar and broke the skin on my throat and I had to have a hepatitis shot and eight stitches.

"Maybe you are not getting the nutrition that you need," I said to him.

The Rodent screeched some Vietnamese lingo at me that sounded like boxcars taking a tight curve. He had to be locked up in the bus toilet for two days and his food shoved in through the louvers, and when we let him out he was still livid, calling me a girly boy, challenging me to fight.

I said, "I am two hundred eighty pounds, Roadie, and you're about seventy-two. No go."

He screamed that I must fight him or else. He said, "I wirr have to hut you bad. I wirr hit you so hod that teals lun down back of neck."

I told him he ought to get into some kind of stress management program, perhaps the YWCA was offering one.

He threatened to take a coat hanger and remove my appendix with it.

I said I was glad that his mother was not there to see him this way, that she would not be proud.

He said, "I reave touw tomollow, Big Boy, but my eyes forrow you, and someday I find you, and wun out of dockness when you reast expect—I fry at you and bite thwoat and kirr you and have you stuffed and mounted and shipped to Hong Kong well you wirr stand in entwance of my westauwant, The Prace of the Wat."

I said, "Rodent, it is only a sport. I am sorry if your feelings were hurt. I am an American. Irony is our birthright. We are a nation of kidders."

He said, "You not my bwuthel no mole. You make me rooze face. I fear onry wage in my hot. Wage that wirr never be assuaged untir I kirr you."

And then I made the mistake of laughing out loud. It struck me as so cute that foreigners use words like "assuage."

That laugh had no sooner left my lips than the Rodent leaped snarling at me. I was quicker this time and I caught him before his incisors got hold of my throat and I hoisted him in the air, his arms and legs flailing, spit dripping from his rage-twisted lips, and I told the driver to pull over. I stuck my old partner head-first in a trash barrel at a scenic

overlook of **Mount McKinley** and turned away. I heard his voice coming from in front of me. (He had that ability to throw his voice.) He said, "Big Boy, I wirr forrow you forevel untir one day you werax and drop god. I wirr watch you as a cat watch a cwippered chickadee. And to wemind you, I wirr reave you **a wed wose.**"

CHAPTER 14

LACY

I found The Rodent's first red rose three years later the night I laid eyes on the woman of my dreams, my adorable Lacy, the night I was dancing onstage at the St. Paul Civic Center as chief of security for Led Zeppelin on their Beautiful Killers tour.

I had been wrestling every winter for Felix up north and getting good and sick of bus rides, and I was doing my "Calling Big Boy" show on a Twin Cities radio station, a two-hour daily gripefest, but the gig with Limp Blimp was the highlight of my year. Jimmy Page, Robert Plant, John Bonham, and John Paul Jones were the Formula One band of all time, rock 'n' roll in a bottle, and if you don't know that, then you weren't there. You were a **Beatles** fan, weren't you?

GHOST:

Yes, I was.

I thought so. It shows. The **Beatles** were all very winsome and cute and geniuses at marketing themselves, but they were **a banjo band** compared to Zeppelin. The Zep had the bull by the tail. The Zep was what justified white guys stealing licks from black guys in the first place. The **Beatles** were for **English majors.** They were to rock 'n' roll what you are to a Walrus, writer boy. What lemonade is to sulfuric acid. What gay men are to Gaelic.

It was a June night and 18,500 Zepsters were grooving to the sound of raw power, at a volume level that cut open your brain, and I was pumped, I was boogeying onstage and picking up crashers and tossing them back into the mosh pits and suddenly there she was in the crowd, impossibly lovely, in tight jeans and a green silk shirt, riding around on a guy's shoulders and throwing her long auburn hair in figure-8s. The sight of her made my heart pound and the Zep faded into the distance, like a smelting plant when you get in your car and drive home. **BOOM.** She blew me away.

I dashed out the door the minute the band was safely off-stage and in their limos, and I stood in front of the arena looking around for her. Meanwhile the fans spotted me. (I was wearing red-striped **Spandex tights** and neon green shades with **flashing pink rims.**) They were crawling up my back for autographs and wanting their pictures taken with me, the 300-pound dancer, and then I got a glimpse of her in a distant parking lot as she ducked into a green Volvo. Oh

darling. I darted across the street in front of a flotilla of Harleys as the Volvo pulled out of the lot and turned west on Seventh Street and I grabbed onto the last Harley and hopped on behind a big black leather jacket with Shogun hair and he said, **"Where to, bro?"**

I said, **"Follow that green machine."**

We followed her about two miles, ran a red light, and suddenly **WHOOOO** this kid darts out in front of us and we swerve **EEEEEEEEEEEEEEEEE** and bounce over a curb and onto a newly sodded lawn and Shogun is fighting to keep her upright and we go fishtailing between these two houses and into the backyard and there's a wedding! beside a rock garden! a fountain! women in white dresses! guys in tuxes! we go careening up the mound of rocks through the flowers, people flying left and right like chickens, and **BWANGGGG** knock the fountain off and **VRRROOOOMMMMM** he guns the bike and we blow past the priest and through a privacy fence and hang a right and get back on **Seventh** and go racing west 60 m.p.h. past the brewery heading toward the airport, me trying to pick the bridal bouquet out of my face, passing cars left and right, then I spot her turning onto Lexington and I point and Shogun cuts through a playground, through a wire fence and the infield of a Little League game, parents screaming at us, and six blocks later we roar up behind her and God bless her, she jams on the brakes—Oh darling— and the bike flips and Shogun hits the asphalt and I go high, headfirst across the roof and do a full somersault on the hood and wind up hanging onto the bumper as she comes to a stop. Then I let go and lay back on the pavement and closed my eyes.

She threw herself down beside me and said, "Oh my God" about thirty times and when I could feel tears under my eyelids I opened them and looked up and said, **"I'm in love with you."**

And then saw that she wasn't the woman who was at the concert.

She was, if anything, more beautiful than that woman. She had a perfect chin and green eyes and milky skin and shoulders like melted caramel. There was a soft air-brushed quality about her or maybe it was only the tears in my eyes.

I told her again that I loved her, to see if I meant it, and I did.

> I fell in love with someone at a distance who, close-up, turned out to be someone else. Is that so strange? No. It's the old, old story of love. Ancient, really. But how would you know about that?

GHOST:
Are you talking to me?

I don't see anybody else here.

GHOST:
Go ahead and insult me all you like, but remember, I'm the one with the typewriter, and if I walk out of here,

you'll have to find someone else to write your book, and meanwhile you're out the twenty-five hundred dollars you paid me up front.

The hell I am.

GHOST:
Check the contract. That money's mine.

It is not.

GHOST:
It is.

Is not.

GHOST:
Is so. By the way, that curtain behind you is moving.

Where??

GHOST:
Guess it's only the wind. Tell me about Lacy.

She was astonishingly beautiful. Her name was Lacy Larson. She had a necklace with an *LL* hanging from it. She wore a perfume that smelled like magnolias at high noon with saxophones playing. She brushed the dirt off my head and asked if she should call an ambulance. I said, heck no, and I stood up and sat on the curb. Shogun crawled out from under the car and scooted over to his bike, which had been reconfigured by the trunk of an oak tree. He collapsed next to it, face down in the grass, and sobbed in a manly way. She inquired again about the ambulance.

"This man feels terrible about his bike," I said. "He needs to be left alone. And when he comes to his senses, we don't want to be here. He may speak disrespectfully to you and then I'd have to kill him."

She and I drove off in the Volvo. She asked where I was headed for. "Following you to the ends of the earth," I said. And then I noticed the music emanating from the tape deck: an acoustic guitar, flat, and a reedy woman's voice with that feminist whine and I caught the line, **"We are islands drifting in the sea of life and seldom do our peripheries touch"** and I had a terrible sinking feeling that sank a little more when I saw the book on the dashboard. Doris Lessing. Whoa. And underneath it was one of those blank books with fancy red leather binding they sell in bookstores for English majors to keep their journals in.

"Do you mind if I ask you a personal question?" she said.

Frankly, a woman can't ask too many personal questions for my taste. It's when she already knows the answers that it gets tiresome.

She said, "Why are you wearing those green glasses with flashing rims?"

I told her they were prescription glasses to cure the snow blindness I had suffered that winter in Alaska.

She said, "Anyway, you have nice eyes."

I waited for her to say something nice about the rest of me.

"Can I drop you off somewhere?" she said.

I said, "There's a revolving restaurant downtown. What do you say we give it a whirl?"

She said, "I need to stop for gas first." We pulled into a Superamerica and she got out and pumped and I snuck a look in the red book. Sure enough, it was her journal. For the previous day, June 12, she had written:

> i sit looking out my window at clouds in the sky & feel i am existing in shadows & leading a ghost of a life—so many unanswered questions racing through my mind. so much beauty and yet sadness everywhere. i am longing for something real & true to my heart. perhaps somewhere i shall find the essence of my being. it is a painful search, passing by all the blank lives of people i see everywhere. does no one have the passion i feel deep within my soul? passion for the greatness of life? or am i too one of the blind, an empty vessel never to be filled? can it be true that time heals all wounds? or is bitter laughter to be my fate? the clouds are a constant reminder of the lightness i long for in my soul. to ride happily and peacefully on the wind—

I sat, stunned, looking straight ahead at the windshield. I had fallen in love with a whooping liberal. And there was no way back: Jimmy (Big Boy) has a heart that cannot be reprogrammed. I was in love, period. I hoped that somehow the woman singing about islands in the sea of life could be made to disappear. And I promised myself I would never never look in Lacy's journal ever again. Beyond that, I could only hope for the best.

We drove to the **Zelda Hotel** and rode the elevator up to the **Rotary Restaurant** on top and got a table overlooking the Mississippi. I made a mental note to order the grilled vegetables and skip the gin. As I was pointing out the sights of St. Paul—**Dayton's Bluff,** the **Indian mounds, Holman Field,** the **Robert Street bridge**—I noticed **a red rose** taped to the window beside me. And a note that said, "Watching you, Big Boy."

St. Paul's legendary Hotel Zelda, home of the Rotary Restaurant, where the upper echelon meets to tie on the feed bag

It was taped to the outside of the window.

Then it dawned on me what a relentless perfidious foe I was up against.

A Minnesota woman never tells a man he's wonderful for fear of leading him on, but I got the idea that Lacy definitely liked me, and why shouldn't she, after the creeps she'd known? Her previous heartthrob was **a storyteller** who did renditions of **"How Mr. Moon Got His Face"** and other p.c. bilge, and the one before him was **a seminarian** who, like 90 percent of the dweebs in the world, followed baseball religiously and studied the box scores. How could I fail to impress after yoyos like them? I knew my own mind and said what I thought and didn't care if it made me look smart or not. She asked me once if I had a sense of humor. I told her that what

I promised her a lifetime of burning love. So far, so good.

I lacked in irony, I made up for in stability. "If you want comedy, go to the movies," I said. "If you're looking for a lifetime of burning love, you're looking at him."

By November, when I was due back in Alaska, she and I were engaged to be married in the spring. We made a deal: She would handle all decisions about the house and the kids and I would run my own life and decide what I thought about things. We visited her par-

ents on their farm near Luverne to announce the betrothal. Her mom, Dottie, was a sweetheart, and I overheard her tell Lacy's old man, "If he's good to Lacy, Howard, then that's all that matters." I'm sure she could sense that Big Boy is strictly a one-woman man.

The old man seemed standoffish until I mentioned to him that I was in the oil business. "Maybe so," he said, "but I seen you on television fighting a man in the ring and standing up for the environment and everything."

I looked at him in astonishment that the I.W.W. had been telecast, and he patted me on the shoulder. "I thought you did real well," he said. "It was interesting what you said about protecting wild species for future generations. I couldn't agree more. In fact, I liked it so well I sent in for

one of your action figures." He pointed to the mantel. There was a plastic replica of me as The Flower Child, identical right down to the cleft in the chin.

I packed my tinted glasses and feather boa and hot azalea silk shirt and tangerine beachcombers and codpiece and kissed my darling Lacy good-bye and flew north for the winter tour of the I.W.W., steaming hot under the collar, waiting for a chance to get Felix in a corner. When I landed in Anchorage, there was a message from him saying he'd been delayed in Cancun and that I should take charge. Svend had retired that summer, and Yukon Bob, and Felix had hired a swishy blond named Bryce who reeked of lilac cologne, and an old fatty cakes named Moby Dick, who was fish-belly white and weighed about 900 pounds and had a specially constructed seat on the bus, and a motor-mouth named Al Tomato, and one named Bull Durham whose neck was bigger than his head, and one called, simply, Mr. Desolation.

"My daddy can whip any man alive, and I can whip my daddy," Desolation yelled when he climbed aboard the bus. "I can outrun, outjump, throw down, drag out, and whip any of you. I have downed a Percheron with a left jab to its fore-head and once kicked a 1968 Ford so hard that it fell off its axles. I can bring a man to his knees simply by spitting on him. Avert your eyes, gentlemen, if you wish to keep your courage, for one sight of me will cause you to give up wrestling and enter the ministry."

"Shut up and stuff it," I said, and gave him a hard squint, and he blinked and swallowed and said, "No offense meant," and plopped down in back.

Felix arrived a week later, after we'd put on ten shows and I'd gotten a good idea of the bundle he was earning from the telecasts. He gave me a big grin and held out his oily hand and I put my index finger against his chest and pressed until I could hear his sternum squeak.

"What's this I hear about our wrestling matches being shown in the Forty-Eight on television?" I said.

He played dumb with me. He said, "What difference does it make? You don't have to fight any harder for it being on TV."

I said, "Felix, a person your size should not try to cheat a person my size—it shows poor judgment on your part." I backed him into a phone booth.

He then tried to tell me that he was losing money on the telecasts. "It's only for promotion!" he cried.

I pulled the phone booth off the wall and hoisted it up in the air and shook him like a Martini. I hollered, "You are a hemorrhoid with legs and if I were to eliminate you without leaving a grease stain, I'd be doing the world a huge favor."

When I put the booth down, he was folded up in the bottom. I said, "Felix, I would hate to think of what a lawyer, even one of dull-normal intelligence, could do to you for having sold my image to television without my permission." I pulled the plastic Flower Child out of my pocket and stuck the head up his left nostril. "And this, Felix—this is larceny. You could do time in jail for this. This was not smart of you, Felix."

And thus I became the managing partner of International World Wrestling and set out to build it up into the No. 1 worldwide attraction that it is today.

TOP DOG

I was top dog on that Alaska tour. I got a cell phone and a secretary back in Minneapolis named **Candy.** I assigned Bryce to be The Flower Child and I made Felix bunk with Durham and I took the wedding suite and sat in the front of the bus and counted the gate and talked to Candy on the cell phone. **I made the rules, I wrote the script.** And I started wrestling as Jimmy (Big Boy) Valente.

I patterned him after **James Arness,** Larry of the **Three Stooges, Spiro Agnew,** the **Grand Exalted Potentate** of

The greatest existential wrestler in history

the Zuhrah Shrine, and **Bo Diddley,** taking the best from each. I shaved my head again and powdered my face and wore a red fez festooned with plumes and rubies and spangly tights and a peacock smoking gown and pink chest hair and rose-tinted shades as big as salad bowls and long sparkly earrings. I wore an ermine robe and gold Arabian slippers with curved toes and I carried on in an extravagant manner, like a French count at **Versailles,** bestowing elaborate contempt on my enemies, strewing insults like flowers.

This was a breakthrough for a boy from Minnesota, a state of Lutherans, a people who don't believe in flaunting the goods or fighting to win, they believe in being humbled and learning to accept it. It is not a showbiz state, Minnesota. It is a state of folks in earth tones. I broke the mold.

Every night Jimmy Big Boy sashayed through the crowd, which was struck dumb at the gaudiness and grandeur of me, and I climbed into the ring like a lion mounts a hillock to scan the **Serengeti** for wapiti. I bore a gilded torch aloft in my right hand and when I squeezed the grip, a blue flame blew twenty feet high and a backfire went **BWAMMMM** and I could see the patrons jump, even the drunks, you could see their eyes twitch.

I was the first pyrotechnic artist in professional sports, I was a flaming genius!

Every night it was a Ring of Fire!

I climbed into the ring and circled it, and plenty of people booed and I didn't give a hoot. Hero or villain, bad egg or Boy Scout, it made no difference—Jimmy Big Boy transcended every petty moralistic distinction—I was the first modern existential wrestler.

GHOST:
You were the first what?

You heard me. In the pink tights, from Hollywood, California, the first EXIS-TEN-SHUL WRESTLER OF MODERN TIMES, the most beautiful man in America, Mr. Jimmy . . . Big Boy . . . VALENTE!!!!"

Ain't no face
So pretty as mine.
Lord almighty,
Ain't I fine?

GHOST:
Do you know what existentialism is?

I am the man who **redefined existentialism.** I made it mean what it means today. It means me. The way I am. Jimmyism.

GHOST:
Well, it may not mean that to everyone.

I can't help everyone. I can only help those who want to be helped. I am what I am, purely myself, and I redefined the ring and broke free of all the old stereotypes—

those old hairy-eyed Nazi wrestlers and the ayatollahs and the sneaky Japs and Chinks and, pitted against them, the hillbillies in their beards and bib overalls and the football heroes and the Canadians—Jimmy Big Boy broke through those clichés—I incorporated good and evil into one character!

People saw me, some booed and some cheered, some did both. I was simultaneously approved and despised. People loved me for the moral ambiguity.

I strode around the ring, my torch breathing flame, my glitter glittering, and when I had everyone's full attention, I grabbed the microphone away from Felix and I looked my opponent in the eye and I yelled, "You pitiful putrid monstrosity with your slimy skin and scurvy eyes and gangrene grin, your face like a water buffalo's butt, I would rather eat the scabs off a cesspool rat than have to meet a depraved degenerate like you but I will crush you like a louse and give you a shellacking you will not forget and throw you back in whatever feedlot pond you come from, you pie-eyed pervert."

People loved this. It was poetry.

And then I proceeded to demolish the guy.

As managing director of the I.W.W., Jimmy Big Boy was not about to go out and lose matches.

I took on all comers. It was on the posters for every event.

WORLD WRESTLING CHAMPIONSHIP
sanctioned by International World Wrestling
starring
Jimmy (Big Boy) Valente
America's Most Beautiful Man & First
Existential Wrestler of Modern Times
HE WILL TAKE ON ALL COMERS
NO EXCEPTIONS
NO HOLDS BARRED

One night in **Point Barrow,** I wrestled a 1,200-pound grizzly
bear. It took place in an airplane hangar packed with six
thousand fans, most of them soaking drunk, and the ring
illuminated by four landing lights stripped from a crashed
B-52, and "The Star-Spangled Banner" sung by a soprano
who sounded as if she were walking across hot coals, and
Felix yelled "Jimmy (Big Boy) Valente" and I paraded out in
my resplendent fez and spangly tights and headdress and
carrying my torch, and the grizzly, a female, about eight feet
tall, honey-colored, sat in a corner of the ring. The look in
her eyes was pure hatred. I climbed in the ring and she
stood up and then I noticed that the leash that was holding
her is chewed off and so is the leg of the guy who was holding the leash. The ring is soaked with blood and the fight
hasn't even begun!

I grabbed the microphone from Felix, who was glad to
relinquish it, and I yelled, "This is it! I'm sick of bears! Sick
of tolerating them! Sick of making excuses for them! Bears
that come after tourists at Yellowstone or Yosemite, that
enter campsites and maul children, that go after hikers—

and what do we do? We blame it on the victims! I say, let's send a message to the bears. Let em know: We're here and we fight back! And that's what Big Boy is going to do tonight!"

The bear listened to this. Then she squatted and let loose an immense volume of steaming bear urine in the ring. Every drunk in the joint was standing and screaming at the top of his lungs, and I walked over and slapped her across the snout. Twice. Then she lunged for me.

I eluded her for a while, circling her—she was a little slow moving clockwise—and I managed to slip behind her and get her in a headlock, and she yanked her head down and flung me into the third row. I climbed back in and waltzed with her again and she tripped me with a paw and slapped me across the ribs and I managed to slither under the ropes and out of the ring and after a couple of minutes, when I finally could inhale again, I jumped back in and popped her in the snoot and got her right arm in a popper hold and we were rasslin' around and I bit her ear, bit it good and hard, and she bellowed and whacked me across the chops so hard I started to remember things I didn't even know I had forgotten. I tried to get her in a clinch. She tried to knee me in the groin. I got her knee and grabbed her under one arm and I hoisted her up and threw her over the ropes into the crowd and boy you should've seen those drunks scramble. The bear was floundering around in the folding chairs and I climbed up on the turnbuckle and I roared my Wild Man roar at her and she roared back at me and lumbered back into the ring and got me in a hug and we waltzed around awhile and then she whispered, **"What do we do now?"**

I said, "Get ready to spit blood because I'm going to get you in the Spinal Snap," and I hoisted her up so she lay across my shoulder on her spine and I jounced her a few times and she screamed and spat blood and a man from the **SPCA** ran into the ring and I coldcocked him with a flying mule and grabbed the bear by one paw and flung her head-first into the turnbuckle and she turned toward me and opened her immense jaws and inside was Al Tomato, his mouth full of ketchup, and I grabbed a shotgun and fired three blanks and the bear went down spouting blood and was dragged away.

The fans looked up at me, sweaty and blood-soaked, smoking rifle in hand, and they screamed and yelled for ten minutes and then slowly filed out, looking like death on toast, facing three more months of winter, and I returned to my suite at the hotel, and there was a call from **Mr. Buzz Waverly** at **Waverly Cable Communications** in **Costa Mesa.** He had seen the show on TV that night. He thought it was the greatest thing since frozen waffles.

"Big Boy, let me tell you where I'm coming from. As I see it, we live, we suffer, we die, and who cares? Nobody. In another ten billion years, earth will be incinerated and become a thin vapor of subatomic particles. So you may as well earn some major money in the process.

"Big Boy, we're going to get the I.W.W. into every cable market in the country, plus **Europe, South America, Japan, Australia.** It'll be the biggest TV show in history. Videocassettes, clothing, novelties, all of it direct marketed. I see this as an

explosion waiting to happen. You push the boat into the current and away we go. Give me the word and we light the rocket."

As it turned out, he was right on the money.

CHAPTER 16

WORLD DOMINATION

I left Felix to manage the northern operation and I flew to L.A. and assembled the I.W.W. Super Team, choosing from the best of our rival organizations, the A.W.A., the W.W.A., the T.W.A., and the W.W.W. I told the guys, "I'm taking over wrestling. Forget about the competition. Join me or find another line of work." And I got the best, the meanies de la meany:

- A 400-pound hunk named Hump Hooley, the master of the Atomic Somersault and the Handshake from Hell.
- Vicious Eddie the Mohawk Kid, with a zipper implanted in his cheek which he unzipped so everyone could see the food in his mouth. Usually it was raw hamburger and egg yolk. **Definitely demented.**
- Big Messer, a.k.a. The Messenger of Death, a.k.a.

Mephistopheles. Not the brightest lantern in the barn but his eyes were set very deep in his head and he could give you fifteen minutes of utterly wacko nonstop barbaric violence and go berserk and commit unspeakable atrocities better than anybody.

- The Widowmaker, who ran around in a black hangman's mask, whacking guys with two-by-fours and lead pipes and sledgehammers, wreaking carnage and hee-hawing like a jackass.

- Speedy Gonzalez (The Bogota Booger), an ocher-skinned greaseball in tight black pants and high-heel flamenco shoes, a master of the coercive arts.

Mr. Disaster. His hair grew six inches per day; you could actually watch it grow.

- Mr. Disaster, who had the brains of a pop-up toaster and biceps as big as bread boxes and weird hair like he had reached puberty near a nuclear power plant, who entered the ring, his body smeared with gore, his right hand bandaged, carrying the head of a woman and assorted

viscera, and went after his opponent with robotic purposefulness.

- Our hillbilly, Blind Boy Butterworth (The Mountain of Muscle, The Colossus of Clout), who wore dark glasses and had a German shepherd named Moon Pie and liked to whip opponents with his white cane and stand atop them and yodel.

- A yuppie bad boy named Brent Beige, who wore **Calvin Klein** white briefs and brought his cell phone in the ring and sat sullenly on a rattan stool and phoned his stylist and complained bitterly about his hair; meanwhile the crowd was begging his opponent to mess him up real bad.

- Dave the Postal Worker, a quiet guy who bore a certain amount of punishment and then erupted beautifully into a maniac and wrought scenes of hideous suffering, dismemberment, et cetera.

- A pointy-headed journalist named Todd Kafka who we had to retire after one bout, people didn't want to see or hear him, he was creepy, like you. Talking about you.

    GHOST: I heard you.

- Me. The Boss. The headliner. Mr. Magnificent.

I gathered the Dream Team together before our first show and I told them, "Boys, you're artists. And art means creating **bold brilliant strokes of color** in a dull gray world. You and I are going to make **great art** that brings happiness to millions, and let's not hold back or be coy. The folks have paid their money, so let's put the show out there where they can get a thrill from it."

Gone forever were the days when two hefty bubbas grappled in the ring and one pinned the other and the referee held the winner's arm aloft and everybody went to the dressing room.

I brought wrestling into the modern age.

I told the guys that we were going to fight according to the theory of relativity. Energy equals mass times the speed of light squared. Which means that there's a gigantic amount of energy even in a very tiny piece of matter such as the brain, for example.

The nature of reality is curved. It isn't a straight line. Time and motion are relative. So be team-oriented, quality-conscious, negotiate power relationships horizontally, and be proactive. That was how we revolutionized wrestling.

We played every major city, always the biggest arena in town, and we stayed on the road for twelve years and earned hundreds of millions of dollars.

We were the Christians entering the Colosseum, and we were also the lions who ate them. We played to arenas of 90,000 screaming fans drinking beer from 40-ounce cups and yelling obscenities I hadn't even heard of yet, their bodies pierced in places I didn't care to know about, throwing lighted cigarettes at us as the arena shuddered to the themes from *2001* and *Star Wars*.

I was the one who introduced real music. In place of the wheezy stadium organ, I brought in killer sound systems

and each wrestler had a theme—mine was **Led Zeppelin**'s "Rock and Roll"—and made his entrance through a cloud of fog and with strobe lights and follow spots and young women throwing themselves in his path.

The Widowmaker swung into the ring from the balcony on an eighty-foot chain and his assistants backed a wood-chipper up to ringside and the Widowmaker liked to throw his opponent into it screaming as blood and gristle flew out. Mr. Disaster rappelled into the ring from the ceiling carrying a ten-gallon cauldron of boiling oil with one hand and doused the ropes with it and when his opponent got the upper hand, Mr. Disaster fished a Zippo out of his crotch and suddenly the ring was an inferno, black smoke billowing, the referee caught on fire, and Mr. Disaster and his opponent climbed together up a steel cable and swung back and forth, trying to dislodge the other and drop him into the holocaust below. The Blind Boy would grope around for his opponent who skulked out of reach and did dastardly things until Moon Pie leaped snarling into the fray and decked the baddie and Blind Boy reached under the ring apron and hauled out a chain saw and revved it up to an ear-splitting scream and the crowd shrank back as he waved it around at the opponent who fought him for control of it and over and over they tumbled, the chain saw ripping the ring and the posts to shreds. Speedy Gonzalez carried a switchblade concealed in the sole of his boot and after the requisite macho strutting and posing whipped out the blade and whirled around like a trapped bird and of course pints and pints of blood were spilled. Vicious Eddie had a hypodermic syringe concealed in *his* shoe sole and displayed it for the audience to see—90,000 people chanting "Needle! needle!" and the ref with no clue whatsoever—and Eddie, palming the syringe, downed his man with a well-aimed scissors kick and immobilized him in a pliers hold and then, with exquisite care, injected him in the middle of the eyeball. Brent Beige, in his moment of crisis, always called for the cops on his cell phone and four heavies in blue lumbered in, waving their sappers, and dispatched the opponent while Brent lounged at ringside, reading the **Wall Street Journal.** Dave the Postal Worker was a clean-cut fellow in blue trunks and a green eyeshade, who wrestled cleanly and scientifically while his opponent pulled one low-down trick after another, rope burns and earlobe lifts and hawkeyes and tongue twists and navel flips, and nipple holds, and finally, unable to restrain himself, Dave opened up one ring post and pulled out a submachine gun and pumped about forty rounds into the opponent as he flopped and flipped around the ring and blood bags burst and then Dave kicked the corpse like a football until security men handcuffed him and removed him from the arena.

I made my entrance from a platform high at the end of the arena, like a high-wire artist. The lights went to black and the announcer cried, "Ladies and gentlemen, the heavyweight wrestling champion of the world—Jimmy (Big Boy) Valente!" and then the spotlight hit me, standing Superman-like, arms at my side, as if about to fly. The **Zeppelin** music hit you like a concrete block and then I raised my arms up

over my head and grabbed onto accordion wire strung taut from the arena wall to the ring below and lowered myself, hand over hand, and when my feet touched the mat, the audience was on its feet screaming. The ring was surrounded by loops of accordion wire. I was the first to use it in place of ropes. Nowadays everyone does that. I was the pioneer.

I was the first wrestler to employ **sweat-seeking cruise missiles** in the ring. When my opponent gained the upper hand and was about to obliterate me, I raised my right fist and took a signal ring off the third finger and opened it and plucked the magic twanger and there was a burst of flame in the rafters and one, two, three, four, five, six giant **Tomahawk** missiles came whirring through the air and slammed into the ring—a flash of flame and big mushroom clouds and when the smoke cleared, my tormentor was burnt toast and I stood, bloodied but victorious in the crisscrossing spotlights.

I hired a press agent, a guy named **Buddy Meadows** who wore burgundy shirts and smoked cigarillos and drove a Buick the size of a coal barge, and wherever the I.W.W. tour went, he got me on the local **Live at Five** newscast—I walked into the studio in my red fez and spangled tights and rose-tinted shades and earrings and I threw some folding chairs around and made **Jim and Jennifer** the co-anchors cower and chuckle uneasily, then I threw **Mike the weatherman** through the map, and I stuck my big face in the camera and yelled, "America is the greatest country in the world and I am the most beautiful man in America, and Hump Hooley, you pukehead, you are nothing but a giant greasy booger in mankind's nostril, and tonight I am going to eliminate you from the face of the earth, you filth." And then I pulled out a

hand grenade and yanked the pin and there was a tremendous din and a burst of orange smoke, and then they cut to a commercial.

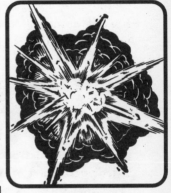

Minutes later, the line began to form at the box office. **Sell Out City.**

I was the man who introduced explosives into pro wrestling, using my Walrus experience to produce maximum whack and minimal harm. We liked to have one wrestler throw another in a Dumpster and then blow it up. We used a monster truck with twenty-foot wheels to crush guys with—backed it up onto a guy's bare belly and spun the tires and listened to him scream. We brought in 10,000-gallon Plexiglas tanks for underwater wrestling, the water pink with blood. And our special effects were the best in the business—wrestlers' heads blown off and brain matter scattered across the mezzanine, raw bleeding flesh, intestines spilling out of gaping abdominal wounds, pulsating organs—our slogan was **Come See Extreme Wrestling—No Children Under Six—Not for the Squeamish—Don't Wear Your Good Clothes** and we lived up to advance billing. After each match, a crew with hoses would sluice down the floor, and another crew would pick up the fainters, and a man with a Vac-Pac would remove the vomit. It got to where we needed six of them.

CHAPTER 17

MINNESOTA CALLS ME

One night in Dallas, a man sat waiting for me in the dressing room. He was glancing at a pictorial feature in *Playboy*, "The Women of NPR," and as I entered, he stood and extended his hand and said, "Jimmy, I am Earl Woofner, the chairman of the Ethical Party of Minnesota. And I've come a thousand miles to say that our state needs a man like you."

Earl Woofner

My skull glittered with sweat, my pink tights were spattered with blood, and I was wearing a peacock-feather headdress, cobalt-blue shades, and a cape with six hundred flashing lightbulbs. Plus, a python draped around my neck. Earl did not flinch.

He set down his briefcase and sat on a bench and looked up at me with complete sincerity. "The people of Minnesota are crying out for a champion to break

the liberal choke hold and open up politics to common sense and honesty," he said. "And I am looking at him."

I took off the glasses and set down the snake.

He said, "I believe that some men receive their true calling later in life, and the calling comes later because it has a nobility and grandeur they could not have appreciated in their youth. And your calling is to bring honest government to the state of Minnesota."

I tried to think of a smart remark and couldn't; for once in my life, I was speechless.

"Me?" I cried.

He stood and put a hand on my shoulder. "What you learned as a Walrus about winning, you've applied to wrestling, and the same can be applied to politics. Winning is a discipline, Jimmy—a habit, if you will. And you are a winner."

I asked him how he knew I was a Walrus.

He smiled patiently. "I know much about you. Your illegitimate birth, your humble origins, your heroic deeds in our country's service, your pursuit of excellence in the entertainment field." He handed me a letter from a woman named **Bernice** who said, "You are a Success in your Chosen Line and now the People are calling you. We your Fans have supported you, Jimmy, and now we need you to support us and throw out the **Special Interests.**" And an envelope containing **a red rose** and a note: "Prease lun for govenol." These were only two of thousands, he said.

He picked up his briefcase and extended his hand. "You will hear more from me shortly."

I pondered his words over the weeks and months and frankly wondered if voters wouldn't be terrified by someone as physically imposing as myself. The layperson seldom confronts wrestlers in day-to-day life, and whenever the Dream Team walks through a hotel lobby or airline terminal, I can sense the astonishment, as if a herd of oxen had stepped off the elevator. Oftentimes I board a plane and sit next to a businessman and he is afraid to initiate a conversation, feeling my 20-inch bicep brushing his shoulder. I open my attaché case and take out the schedule of matches and scribble notes for the scripts—**"Messenger of Death brings guillotine to ring and, while inspecting it, is himself decapitated, and Speedy holds up bloody head and is set upon by feral dogs. Chopper comes. Etc."**—and Mr. Executive Vice-President is eyeballing me but doesn't dare open his mouth and speak: This is the effect we have on people. A 300-pound six-foot five-inch guy is too darn big for normal life. How then could I mingle with voters and win their confidence? And why should I run for public office when I loved the wrestling tour so much?

We wrestlers always flew first class, being too bulky for tourist seats. Stretch limos everywhere, and a beautiful buffet in the dressing room, heavy on prime rib and lamb and mashed spuds, and the hotels were four-star, and we always destroyed our rooms when we left, as a point of honor. Never checked out without at least dropping some cherry bombs into the toilet. We patronized only the best restaurants, and sat and listened to a waiter named Stephen describe the watercress soup, the sprout sandwich on seven-grain, the lentil-tofu soufflé with deviled parsnips, and then we'd each order the forty-seven-ounce beef butt with french fries and a quarter-pound chocolate barge loaded with hot fudge and ice cream for dessert.

The tour was good to us. And when my guys got moody, I was there to gin them up.

Once, backstage at the **Kingdome** in **Seattle,** with 50,000 fans in the seats, Speedy put his head in his hands and said, "I can't do it, Big Boy. Speedy is done."

He said that the smoke and fire and lasers and loud music were getting on his nerves and he couldn't sleep at night. Besides that, he had committed his life to the Lord and couldn't see how wrestling served the Kingdom of God.

"Listen to me," I said. "Those little people out there in the dark, they need you and me and Hump and Messer and all of us. They work in an economy based on **specialization,** in which they're **interchangeable parts,** and they live in apartment complexes **interchangeable** with ones in Houston or Atlanta or Phoenix, and what they miss more than anything is pure chauvinism, which is anathema in the economy because it hinders productivity, but people miss it, that old atavism, the blood lust, and living in a society of anonymity among the **Burger Kings** and **Barnes and Nobles,** they need **hatred** to give them a sense of belonging, and that's where we come in—me and Meph and Mr. Disaster and you, Booger—we're metaphors and icons, a beacon in their dim lives, creators

of moral fables! Can't you see it? They need us, the Kingdom of God needs us, and we're not going to let them
down!"

And we didn't. The blood flowed, the monster truck
roared and the chain saws, the ring burst into flames, death
and destruction rained down, the missiles came whistling
in, and the fans went away happy.

CHAPTER 18

THE STRONG MAN

Earl Woofner stayed in touch. He sent clippings about the
excesses of government to get my blood boiling. And how
the special interests lounged around on public largesse.

Special interests
lounging

And he passed along notes from Min-
nesotans of all walks of life hoping I
would run for governor. He also clued
me in to a beautiful thirty-acre tract
along the **Mississippi** north of **Minneapolis,** in the suburb of **Poplar Bluff,** and I
bought it for a song and built a beautiful house for Lacy and me and the
kids, a house with a hundred mirrors and a swimming pool
the shape of my head and the driveway lit with gas torches.

I bought Gladys a big white rambler in **Edina** for her twilight years. She said, "All I want, Clifford, is to know that
you and your sisters are enjoying the finer things of life that

I learned to do without." She told me she hoped I would find a new career where I wouldn't have to kick people. She said that Eunice and Arvonne missed me and that Arv had asked about me several times—he had moved back to **Minneapolis** minus the hygienist, and he and Gladys were good friends and members of a square dance club, **The Jolly Trotters.**

I wasn't around Minnesota much. Lacy raised the kids. I missed a lot of birthdays and school concerts and soccer games, and then when I was around, they weren't always that glad to see me. When I drove Adrian to grade school, he asked me to drop him off a block away, he wasn't anxious to be seen in the company of a 300-pound bald man with green rhinestone glasses.

"But I'm your dad," I pleaded.

"You are about as attractive as a pustule on the butt of a dying rhino," he replied.

That's when I put my foot down: No more watching Daddy on TV.

It was thrilling every year when World Championship Wrestling came to **Los Angeles** and we played the **Rose Bowl** and went all out on the bombs and flames, and we could see Tom Cruise and Bruce Willis and Sly Stallone in the front row on the fifty-yard line, eating it up and taking notes. I always sent complimentary tickets to Arnold's office, along with a gift certificate for a limo service, and year after year his seats were empty, and then one year he was there, in a seal-skin jacket, waving to me.

I stood on a tiny three-by-four platform at the top of the bowl end, a hundred feet above the crowd, and even with the spotlight in my face I could see Arnold in the front row, staring up at me. I thought, *Take a good look, Mr. Movie Star, and see a man do a dangerous stunt with no re-take!* I raised my fists in the air, and just then I heard a harsh voice behind me yell, "Rots of ruck, sucka!" and a hard little hand shoved me and I grabbed for the razor-sharp accordion wire just as I fell off the platform and the crowd gasped and I lowered myself quickly to the ring, hands dripping blood, and I looked at Arnold and he had fainted and two women were waving damp towels over him.

Afterward, he came to the dressing room and we talked. He said he remembered me from **Cam Ranh Bay,** a lie, but I appreciated the gesture. He said he loved the show and I ought to think about making movies someday. So that night I sat down in my hotel suite and wrote a 110-page script called *Strong Man.*

GHOST:
You wrote a script yourself?

Writing is nothing. If you can think straight, you can write. It took me eight hours. One draft, no corrections. Arnold told me he never saw a script as professional as mine.

GHOST:

I had no idea you wrote.

There's a lot you don't know. If I had the time to do it, I'd write my own life story and it'd be three times as good as what you're doing.

GHOST:

What's wrong with the way I'm writing it?

You can't get the poetry of my life. The sensibility. The shadows. You can only know me as a palooka. You're missing out on the loneliness of the big man.

GHOST:

So tell me about it.

I'm not the kind of guy who talks about that stuff.

GHOST:

Then how am I supposed to write it?

If you don't know, then you're nothing but a stenographer.

GHOST:

Let's get back to the story.

You know, the problem with you is that you never went out on the edge. You never had to go to **Alaska** and face

up to yourself. You took the easy out and went for the vicarious life hearing about other guys' lives so you'd never need to find one of your own and now here you are, fifty-six, glum, broke, angry at the world, and on top of it you're not that bright. Because there is no substitute for personal experience, mister. You can never be truly happy unless you've been out on the edge and heard the sirens sing and found the weirdness and insanity of the world. I've been there. All you've been to is a bunch of used book stores.

GHOST:
You're a very unpleasant man, Governor.

I can be even more unpleasant if push comes to shove. Don't push me.

GHOST:
Let's get this over with. I don't want to talk to you.

Then shut up and listen, goomba.

I wrote this pellucid script called *Strong Man*. It was about **Heracles,** the love child of **Zeus** by **Alcmene,** so Zeus's wife, **Hera,** was naturally miffed over the existence of Heracles and caused him to go insane and murder his own children. When he recovered his sanity, he went to **the oracle at Delphi** to seek instructions, and was told that if he performed these **Twelve Labors,** he would become immortal. He had to kill **a giant lion** and **a monster with nine heads** and capture a ferocious **boar** and clean out **a king's stable** in one day and eliminate some **giant man-eating birds** and capture a **fire-breathing bull** and also **four savage horses** and get a golden girdle away from the **Amazons** and get some cattle away from **Geryon,** a three-headed man who was the strongest man alive, and steal golden apples from Hera's tree guarded by a dragon named **Ladon** and then trot down to **Hell** and cross the River **Styx** and capture the hell-hound **Cerberus.** There is a lot of action for 110 pages.

The next day I handed it to Arnold's agent **Larry** and sat in his office full of ficus plants while he read it.

"Is this finished or is this an early draft?" he asked.

But Arnold loved it. He paid me $125,000 for it and put it into development. Arnold told me, "Quit wrestling, it's bad for your back. You have a gift. Come to Hollywood and in four years, maybe six, you'll be a major star. A star like **Willem Dafoe** or **John Malkovich.** A **Christopher Walken."** It hurt that he put me in that company and not with Willis and Stallone. I saw Stallone play Rambo and it was like seeing a child play Chopin. Six months later Arnold sends me a rewrite of *Strong Man* and it's been retitled *Terminator 2: Judgment Day.* Completely destroyed it. "Moviemaking is a collaborative process," he told me.

I thought, *Sure, like kidnapping. You can't do it without a kidnappee.* He then offered me a small part in his next film, that of a cowboy soldier, and I took it, as a favor to him, and it was a nothing part. One line. **"I'm too busy to die."** That was it. Five words.

I was on the set, shooting my one tiny line over and over about a hundred times, with Arnold directing me, offering helpful tips like **"Pull it back more so it comes more from within yourself"** and **"Let it out a little and give it some breathing room"** and **"Now let's take it in a new direction and play with the irony."** He tortured me like I was a cat.

Before the 101st take of my line, the makeup girl came over to touch up my face. She said, "I love watching you work, you're such a pro." I said **thank you** and suddenly she was snarling, hissing, chewing on my throat, and her wig came off—The Rodent! It was all I could do to pry his jaws off me. Everyone on the set treated it like a big joke.

So of course they used the 101st take in the movie, the one where I was practically in shock, and all the reviews described my acting as "wooden"—Lacy said, "It depends on how a person feels about wood. And what kind of wood. Personally I love birch and maple." But the reviews depressed the heck out of me.

I told Arnold that the critics upset me, and he (who, by the way, was universally hailed for his work in a film that I got no screenwriting credit for) told me, "Forget the critics. Keep working at your acting and in six years, maybe eight, you'll be another **Dan Baker** or **Jack Irwin.** Another **Paul W. Hoffman.**"

He recommended a guru to buck me up, an Indian named **Rabindranath Janarandamahakrishnamurti** who worked out of a back room at the **Shalimar Restaurant** on Sepulveda, a diminutive mystic who looked up from a plate of tandoori lentils and advised me to practice serenity and to see with the inner eye and to locate within myself the warm glowing disc of divine love that is at the center of all creation. To facilitate energy flow, he showed me how to do a three-point yoga headstand. And when I was all balanced, he shrieked and tore off his dhoti and went for my throat! The Rodent again. I fell on top of him and he yelped and squirted out from under me and turned and tried to kick my face off, missing by millimeters, and I caught his foot and held on and swung him like a cat and threw him out the window and into the parking lot, where he slunk off through the silver BMWs like a whipped cur.

I yelled, "Get a life!" And he yelled back, "You my rife, Varente!"

I called Arnold sixteen times from my hotel in **Beverly Hills,** and finally he took the call, and sort of apologized, and I told him I didn't trust him or anybody else in Hollywood.

"You wouldn't want me on your jury, Arnold," I said. "I was brought up by Lutheran people and taught to be charitable, as Luther says in the **Small Catechism,** to speak well of your neighbor and explain his actions in the kindest possible way, but Luther didn't know anybody in Hollywood. If Luther'd known movie people, he would've put more emphasis on eternal damnation."

Arnold said that he considered me a close personal friend.

I said, "I'd like to be, but we're not there yet because in

your mind Jimmy Big Boy is a bit player and not a creative force. Maybe if I got elected governor of Minnesota, you'd start treating me with a little respect."

He laughed so hard at that, it hurt my feelings. I slammed down the phone and yanked it from the wall and threw it out the window onto **Rodeo Drive.** And my eye fell on a note that Earl Woofner had sent me that very morning: "It is time for Heracles to come home and clean the stables."

CHAPTER 19

JIMMY COMES HOME

I was sitting on top of the wrestling world, the I.W.W. Heavyweight Champion, in the spotlight, cheered by the biggest crowds ever assembled and earning millions, chumming around with Hollywood stars, getting a million hits a day at **jimmybigboy.com,** and the constant acclaim made me a little tense and irritable, knowing that one day stardom would come to an end. How much longer could I continue whaling on people and pounding the birdseed out of them and calling in cruise missiles and destroying them? And what would I do afterward?

When you're young, you believe in magic, like in fairy tales, where you solve a riddle put to you by a beggar and suddenly an owl flies down from a tree with a gold ring in its beak and you rub it and a genie appears who grants you three wishes, but as you get older and you keep solving riddles put to you by beggars and all they do is spit on your shoe, you figure it out:

1. We are not heroes.
2. Our time here is brief.
3. Our untapped potential is limited: We are doing about the best we can do.
4. Personal charm doesn't count for much.
5. There's no point in looking back. It doesn't help.

Life is short, and nobody is a winner for long. You win the golden trophy, you hold it high in the air and thank your fans and grin at the camera, the champagne dripping from your chest hairs, and the next day you start the long grim slide down the garbage chute. I have seen this happen to wrestlers.

Wrestling gets hard as you pass forty. It is tiring to be around great big wild-eyed sweaty violent people and tiring to meet wrestling fans, a breed that includes many mouth-breathers and people who think **Elvis** is talking to them through the mail slot and women with many interesting tattoos and **Flat Earth** people and men obsessed over the secret covenants of the world **Zionist U.N.**

Your back hurts from all those 300-pound guys you've hoisted up over your head and twirled around in the Helicopter and heaved into the seats. Your knee cartilage goes to pieces. Your shoulders get stiff. Bone spurs sprout every-

where. You give up doing your curls and crunches and lateral raises and your super-sets get smaller and soon you gain eighty pounds and become a big fat washed-up Has Been getting ready to go down for the long count. You leave the ring and nobody misses you much; younger and faster carnivores take your place. You earn chicken feed doing color commentary and endorsing **ginseng pills** and **hernia belts.** The steroids in your body go bad: Soon, you have the sex drive of a potted plant, your skin withers up and starts to resemble a rotten cantaloupe. You get on that streetcar named **Oblivion** and the next stop is a **VFW** club where you become a pathetic bleary-eyed blimp parked on a bar stool, hands trembling, letting guys buy drinks for you. One day, **a software salesman** nails you with a lucky punch and you lose your balance and fall and hit your head on the stool and now you can no longer remember your **Social Security** number.

It was a depressing prospect.

I was in Cleveland, a depressing town to begin with. I called up Lacy and told her I was feeling down and she said she was reading a book about aging that said it isn't a crisis, it's an opportunity to enjoy new possibilities in your life.

The new possibility she had in mind was a property on **Maui.**

So I bought it for her. It's on the ocean so the kids can surf and sail. We named it Jimmyville. I love Minnesota but I don't enjoy it all that much, especially in November, when the sky fills up with clouds like piles of dirty laundry and the temperature falls and you go into a tunnel for six months. Jimmyville is our paradise.

I hired Svend the Yellow-Toothed to take care of it for me. I ran into him a few years ago in a bar at **O'Hare,** his golden locks dirty, his blue eyes rheumy and glazed, snarfling up whiskey sours like they were cream sodas. I gave him a job on **Maui** and a cottage and soon he was back on his feet again. The week after he sobered up, he sent me e-mail:

> **Jimmy, the fog has lifted and I am smelling the roses again because you saved my life and now you have a friend forever. No matter what, I am in your corner. May I give you a word of advice? Retire. Bring the wife and kiddoes out here and enjoy the fruits of your labors. You will love Hawaii. The people are pleasant, not like those bitter pills of Minnesota. You belong here where you will be loved, which will never happen in Minnesota. They are not capable of it. A word to the wise.**

And then suddenly I got into politics. I was back home and some Walrus buddies and I met for a few beers in a topless club called **The Office,** about a mile from my house, and on the way out we had to walk a gauntlet of **old-lady liberals in brown oxfords** carrying signs that said **"Would you want your daughter to work here?"** and yelling "Shame!" at us, and when we drove away, the rearview mirror was suddenly full of flashing blue lights. The cops checked my brake lights and muffler and turn signals and my license and said I was speeding.

"What sort of speed laws are these?" I said. "Is this an Amish community? Where are the buggies?"

They told me not to get smart.

"I would think you boys could find better things to do than sandbag a group of American veterans," I said.

"This is a nation of laws," they replied.

"It is also a nation of common sense. And we both know that if those waitresses in there had been wearing U of M sweatshirts, you wouldn't be out here inspecting mufflers."

"It is not uncommon for miscreants to blame society for their misdeeds," they said.

"I do not blame society," I said. "I blame the municipal government, and I shall see that the rascals are duly thrown out."

I filed my candidacy for mayor the next morning and campaigned on the slogan **"Free to Be Yourself"** and promised that citizens would no longer be harassed for burning trash in the backyard or letting dogs run loose or building a garage the way they wanted it or playing loud music when you have a patio party in the summer or painting the house your favorite shade of purple and adding flashing pink lights around the windows or riding a jet ski up and down the river at 11 p.m. or whenever it darn pleases you to ride it.

"It is no function of government to harass a person for a little innocent pleasure," I said.

I won 70 percent of the vote, and my sweet Lacy said, "Does this mean you are retiring from the ring?"

"No," I said, "I promised the people less government, not more, and providing less government is not a full-time job."

She said she wished I would retire for her sake, she was scared to death I would be killed by a cruise missile.

"I am earning too much money to retire," I said. "And the job is less dangerous than that of a clown in the circus."

CHAPTER 20

JIMMY'S MIDLIFE CRISIS

One night in the **Boston Garden,** Hump Hooley and I fought a marathon tag-team match against The Messenger of Death and Mr. Disaster, a real butt-burner involving quarts of blood, thousands of vampire bats, a pack of rabid wolves, six suicide bombers from **Hamas,** and twelve Tomahawk missiles, and in the finale I hoisted The Messenger over my head and heaved him into the turnbuckle only to have him ignite a moat of gasoline around the ring and I passed out from the fumes and lay unconscious, the flames licking at my feet, death near at hand—and then excruciating pain awakened me! I leaped up and called in an air strike on myself! The cruise missiles came straight at me! **SMOKE AND FLAMES! UTTER CONFUSION!** And when the smoke cleared, there was a heap of ashes in the middle of the burning ring where I had been! The crowd screamed, "No! No! Not Big Boy!" And then I jumped up and brushed the ashes away and **Old Glory** descended from the rafters and I took hold of a corner and was lifted to safety as the ring exploded and burned.

When the match was done, I lay on the dressing room floor, too tired to shower. The Messenger of Death brought me a beer and Hump helped me into a chair. I glanced at myself in a mirror and was shocked at the grayness and blankness of me, the fatuous look in the eyes, as if I were on powerful medications. Or else as if I wasn't and should be. I looked like a snake who had swallowed a dog.

"Loved the flag bit," Hump said. "Write that into the act from now on."

I said, "Boys, I believe I need a vacation."

In the morning I went to a doctor, who diagnosed a nasty case of testosterone poisoning. The pills I took to keep my energy up were causing a diabolic vasodilation of the nerve endings. I was getting numb above the neck.

I called Lacy and she said, "Jimmy, just say the word and I'll take you to paradise. We'll eat fresh fruit and ride horseback in the surf and make love in a bed strewn with flowers. I could make you very happy," she said. She had that sweet tone in her voice that women get when they're about to talk you into something, the sweet anticipation that of course you're about to say yes.

"I have a dream," I said.

"Wake up from it," she replied.

I was sinking and I knew it from all the sharks attracted to me, mutual fund salesmen and development directors, **Tank Baldwin** wanted to sell me a Lincoln, old Walrus buddies called with ideas of starting mink ranches or opening a restaurant called **Mama's.** Arv sent a long teary letter and two western adventure manuscripts, **Possibly Serious Injuries** and **A Man Alone Somewhere in the Rockies,** both equally unreadable, that he hoped I'd find a publisher for. I called Earl.

Abe Lincoln, another rassler in politics

"Minnesota needs you," he said. "Franchise joints are taking us over, massive hog farm operations, casinos sucking the loose change out of the senior citizens, little towns drying up, former 4-H-ers heading for the Cities in their sheer blouses and push-up bras, everybody looking to hit the jackpot and nobody remembering to raise the kids.

"In the Cities, you have parents attending to their careers, networking, managing their investments, nourishing their inner selves, having abandoned their children to electronic devices. So the kids know everything about the Internet and *The Simpsons* and don't know who **Abe Lincoln** was and don't care, have no conception of Memorial Day, not even the faintest interest.

"Meanwhile, at the Capitol, lobbyists are aswarm like bees on spilled pop. The agribusiness boys are calling the shots, and the teachers' union, everybody angling for a loophole, to get a spot at the head of the trough, everybody except the little guy, who, as usual, has to settle for the short end. The little guy who the Ethical Party is sworn to uphold."

"What about it, Jimmy?" he said. "The troops are ready. When do we get the order to march?"

I sat one morning in **Al's Breakfast Nook** in southeast **Minneapolis,** and it burned my bacon, just to think about politics.

By rights I should be a Democrat, because I am for the little guy, but the Democrats are run by yuppie liberals trying to remake American society into a day-care center for adults. Making folks stand outdoors to smoke a cigarette. Making a teacher fill out a fourteen-page questionnaire if she says boo to a kid. Labels on beer cans warning that alcohol is not good for your health and may cause you to fall down on the floor.

The Democrats started out with the **NEW DEAL,** a good idea for its time, and then delusions of grandeur led them to keep adding onto it, like a guy who sets out to make carbonara sauce and starts throwing sausage and peppers and onions in and pretty soon you've got hearts of palm and peas and anchovies and water chestnuts and pineapple swimming around in it and the thyme and oregano are at toxic levels and nobody is hungry anymore. That's the Democratic platform. Programs for everything—programs to combat grumpiness, stupidity, discrimination, covetousness, improper lane changes, low math scores, flat beer, poor taste, too much air in the Cracker Jack box, and all of the programs require battalions of social workers and reams of paper.

So I look to the Republicans, and what do I see? The **Screw You** Party: Squeeze the maximum profit out of everything, strip it clean, gouge what you can, clear-cut the forest, to hell with everybody else— lay off the twenty-year guys and hire cheap replacements, cut costs, inflate the stock, sell out, make your pile, leave town, head for your compound in Palm Springs, buy an electronic security system and a team of Rott- weilers, sit around the swimming pool, enjoy your brains out, and feel no more remorse than a fruit fly.

So here I am in the Ethical Party, a grab bag of bikers and bird-watchers and disgruntled dishwashers and surly seniors and people who call in to talk shows to bitch about the mailman.

CHAPTER 21

JIMMY MAKES A MOVE

The waitress at Al's slid the platter in front of me, the Cajun omelet on home fries with a side of sausage, and there was **a rose** stuck in the sausage. I opened the newspaper and written in red crayon across the top of the sports page was **You lun, you rooze.**

That was the expert wisdom a year ago.

Buddy Meadows planted an item in the Minneapolis *Star Tribune*, **"Wrestler Ponders Statehouse Bid,"** and the next day all the columnists cackled over it as if I were a baboon wearing a hat.

Earl Woofner sent me a computer-generated picture of me in a suit and tie, standing on the Capitol steps, between two rows of state troopers saluting smartly. It looked good, I gotta admit.

"We have to talk," Lacy said that night. The four words that strike fear into a man's heart.

She told me to make up my mind. Run if I was going

My Porsche. This baby can go.

to run, and if I didn't get elected, we'd go to Hawaii. And if I won the election—she smiled, she didn't figure that was a real possibility.

It was May, 1998. I took a week off from the tour and got in my Porsche with the **Mess with the best, die with the rest** bumper sticker and took a run around Minnesota. Drove for a day and a half, Minneapolis to International Falls to Moorhead to Worthington to Winona and home. I prefer the gravel roads where you can make time, roads that would shake your fillings out at 30 but at 140 you fly over the bumps like melted butter. From Moorhead to Worthington, on some of those straight stretches, I held it at 200 for a while, a speed that would make you wet your pants, mister, but I think better when I'm moving fast.

I cruised the state and I pondered the future.

A state of severe contrasts, bust and boom. Outstate, farmers in hock and going broke, having bought fancy

combines at 20 percent interest and now the price of corn was bottoming out and the loans were coming due, and in the Cities, the factories had moved to South Carolina and the old factory buildings were turned into restaurants serving lamb chops the size of chickadees, plus an artichoke and a small red potato for thirty dollars, meanwhile a bloated state bureaucracy dithered in the face of crisis, formed interdepartmental task forces to locate their own posteriors, held daylong meetings to discuss the effects of excrement impacting a high-speed ventilation device, moved reams of paper, delayed, waffled, marked the years until retirement.

I saw a picture of a candidate for the Democratic nomination for governor, eating tofu at a fundraiser and wearing a T-shirt that said **I really could use a hug right now.** And a picture of a Republican hopeful dedicating a milk-producing plant in which 40,000 genetically engineered Holsteins, heavily sedated and lying on canvas slings and fed with stomach tubes, could produce two million gallons per day.

I stopped in Duluth and spent a few hours running up 40 degree inclines for exercise, and as I did, I called Lacy on the cell phone and asked if she'd ever driven by the governor's mansion on Summit Avenue.

"It looks like the headquarters of an order of Catholic nuns," she said. "Anybody who wants to live in a house like that has got bats in their belfry."

I drove past the abandoned open-pit mines on the Iron

Range on my way to International Falls, on the Canadian border, and took a whiff of the chemicals from the paper plant, and I thought, If I were governor, I'd have to come here and cut ribbons and speak to schoolchildren about citizenship.

Hawaii looked pretty good to me in International Falls. I could live on **Maui,** act in movies, do color commentary on TV, build my net worth, and gradually, gracefully, retire to raising rare orchids.

I drove south to Moorhead and called Earl Woofner. "I can't do it," I said. "I have decided I am not a politician. I don't have the stomach for it."

"That is your strong suit, your honest independent nature," he said. "Sleep on it. Call me tomorrow. The brochure is at the printer's, ready to go. The campaign headquarters is ready to open. The **Jimmy for Governor** beer is bottled, all we have to do is slap on the labels."

I spent the night in Worthington, and I had a dream. I never dream but that night I did.

In my dream, I was on a train late at night, in a coach packed with peasants in baggy pants and billowy blouses, many with chickens on their laps, drinking tea, jabbering in a strange sibilant language. The train kept stopping and more people crowded on and as they did, I got smaller and smaller until I was three inches tall. I had been drinking tea and now I was perched on the saucer as the train jounced along through the dark. We stopped and a bishop in long flowing robes got on and sat next to me and I saw that it was Lenin and the train was crossing the Urals and he was in disguise, trying to escape. I decided to rib him a little. I poked his immense hand. **"From each according to his abilities, to each according to his needs—** they didn't go for it, eh?"

He sighed. **"The people have more opiates than they know what to do with."** We talked on into the night and found that we both loved strawberry ice cream and were fans of Luther Allison and both thought it was nuts that the ball Mark McGwire hit out of the park for No. 70 should be auctioned off for three million bucks by the guy who wound up with it in his hand. Then Lenin got up to go. He reached down and shook my tiny hand and said, **"Now it's your turn. Be ready for it when it is ready to happen."**

Lenin

And then I woke up.

That morning, as I often do when I'm on the road and have an extra minute, I dropped by the local hospital to visit children, and as it happened, there was one, a twelve-year-old boy named Tommy, who had lost his left hand in a corn picker.

"Big Boy," he said, "how can I grow up to become a wrestler without a left hand?"

I told him, "You can be anybody you want to be. Don't ever give up. And it would be a great gimmick. Tommy (The Talon) Anderson. Jump in the ring with your eagle-feather headdress and clack your prosthetic device and get the au-

dience to chant, 'He fought the claw and the claw won.' ' "

He was a chipper little guy with freckles and a big grin, and he looked up at me and said, "How did you become what you wanted to be, Big Boy?"

And I was about to say, "By sheer determination and imagination," and then I thought, *Hey, I'm not there yet. I want to be governor. For once in my life, I want to be taken seriously.* And I looked down at his freckled face on the pillow and said, **"Tommy, I came here to help you out and instead you helped me."**

CHAPTER 22

UP THE COB

I drove east on the Interstate, north of the Iowa border, and spotted a giant corncob looming upright, miles of plowed field around it. I pulled into a parking area, where a sign said *World's Largest Corncob*, and got out and walked up a gravel path toward the cob, which appeared to be about a hundred feet high, made of yellow fiber glass.

I heard a voice say **"Jimmy"** and turned, and a woman in a tight red vinyl outfit stood beside the path. She wore a leopardskin cape and black leather boots halfway up her thighs and black fingernail polish. She had a wild head of hair a guy could get lost in.

"You're coming with me to Ballarat, Jimmy," she said. "It is a planet in the system of Alph in the Creon galaxy, in the realm of Morfar. You can be a klepht."

"Great," I said, stalling for time.

"I like you. You're not like other guys," she said.

"People have told me that."

"Klephts are the warriors of Morfar," she said, "and femors are the workers. You strike me as a warrior."

And then I noticed the big circles in the field, a series of them, each about fifty feet in diameter. And I saw a laser beam snake toward me, and smelled something like chlorine, and looked down and my shoes were smoldering. She stepped toward me.

"Hit me, klepht," she said. "Go ahead. Take a swing. Show your stuff." She stood sticking out her chin, arms at her side.

"I am a gladiator and I cannot strike a woman," I said.

"Make your hand into a fist and hit me. Don't worry about hurting me. You won't."

I shook my head. She put up her fists and danced around me, poking at me. "Come on, Big Boy," she said. "Put up your dukes. Make my day. One on one. Come on, champ." I was scared as a bachelor at a tea dance. "Come on," she said. "Take a swing. Show your stuff. Let's see your best punch."

She was jabbing at me and I put up my hands to ward her off and then she tagged me in the eye with a left jab and came in with a right to the solar plexus and as I was ducking, she caught me with a left-right to the chin.

And then she was snarling, and her wig was off, and it was The Rodent, a machete in one hand and a laser sword in the other.

"The folce not with you, Varente," he said. He circled me, flicking the laser beam toward my throat. He chuckled in his cunning Asian way and spat on the ground. The blade of the machete looked sharp enough to shave a frog's mustache and the laser sword was the real thing: He pointed it at the ground and the grass sizzled. And then I remembered Tank Baldwin's advice: **Go for the legs, get him down, and then kick.**

I gave him the hairy-eye glare, as if he were Pol Pot, and I said, "You've been a stone in my shoe long enough, you freaking idiot," and I went in hard and low and snagged his ankle and he hit the dirt and tried to scuttle away but I was on him, I kneed him in the groin and that took the starch out of him and then I took him by the ankles and swung him around and around and heaved him up, way up to the top of the cob, and he managed to grab on to the tip and hang on, peering down at me, massaging his wrist where I'd twisted it.

"What do you want, Rodent?" I called.

"You expect I ansa that, Varente?"

"What did I do to deserve your devotion?" I sneered.

"What so speciar about you, Varente? Is that what you want know?" he hissed back.

"If I'm not special, why are you trying to drive me out of my mind?"

"Why do it bothel you?"

I looked up at him outlined against the pellucid sky. "You want to know what I really think?"

"Ah you terring me oh asking me?"

"Does it make a difference?"

"You want know what I think of what you think?"

I walked away toward my car. The conversation was going nowhere fast.

I turned and yelled to him, "When I'm elected governor, you're going to wish you'd never left the rice paddies, little buddy. You'll wish you were still looking at the rear end of a water buffalo."

When I got in the Porsche, I felt stiffer than a frog on the interstate. I aimed the hood ornament toward home and called Lacy and told her I had decided to run for governor.

There was a long breath of a pause, and she said, "Fine, but I don't campaign. I don't do the candidate's wife thing at all. Don't do fund-raisers, so don't even ask." I understood, I said.

"Why are you doing this to us?" she asked. I said I was tired of people making fun of me for wearing pink boas.

The car pressed forward. Telephone poles flew by in a blur. The needle was right at 200. "Life is too short to spend it living a lie. Honesty is the prerequisite to any kind of happiness. And wrestling is not honest," I said.

"What about Hawaii?" she said. I pointed out that providing less government would not be a full-time job for me. There would be plenty of time for surfing.

"Do you think you can win?"

"I am a Walrus and I do not lose fights except in fun," I said.

I had the Porsche wound out to 250 now and she was starting to fishtail a little on a country road near **Walnut Grove** as I told Lacy that I would be home in half an hour, and just at that moment a John Deere tractor pulling a manure spreader emerged from a driveway and I had to take the car into the ditch and up in a meadow. She skittered over the rough ground at 220 and I ducked as a strand of barbed wire came guillotine-like across the cockpit, and another, and another, and then she came amidships of a driveway and we were airborne for a moment, and I saw a pile of rocks pass by underneath, and we landed and bounced twice and I steered her back in the ditch and onto the road. Luckily the ditches were shallow and the cows were in the barn.

"Is your car running rough?" she asked.

"She's running a little rough," I said. "But I've got everything all worked out now."

CHAPTER 23

GOVERNOR JIMMY

Buddy Meadows offered to manage my campaign. I said, "Burgundy shirts and cigarillos don't fly in Minnesota, and neither does your taste for tangerine daiquiris. I'm going native." I also told Felix to stay away and Hump Hooley and The Messenger of Death and Speedy Gonzalez, though they all wanted to help out. "Thanks, but no," I said. I got Buzz Waverly to yank the commercials for the I.W.W. World Champion Highlights videocassette, which showed me in pink tights and peacock feathers, mooning Blind Boy Butterworth.

I put on my Australian bush hat, my running shoes, my *Gopher It* T-shirt, and for five months, I rode around Minnesota in a motor home, green, the interior a soft beige that reminded me of the inner thighs of a woman I met once in Miami, and lived on Cheese Doodles, Ho-Hos, and root beer, which gave me so much gas I could hardly keep my socks up, and addressed every Kiwanis club, Elks, Moose, Jaycees, Sons of Norway, Knights of Columbus, VFW, and Eastern Star that cared to hear me, and roamed the coffee shops and Kmarts, handing out literature, pressing the flesh, chewing the fat. Svend drove, looking like an ancient pterodactyl, shrieking at me to give 'em hell and I tried, though it was a tough haul, missing Lacy, who was mad at me for the unliberal things I said, keeping an eye out for the murderous Rodent lurking in the forest of **Big Boy for Governor** placards.

I told the people, "I am not a joke. I am a decent clean person you could bring home and not be embarrassed by. Yes, I wore a pink boa and gave nutcrackers and spinal taps and shin spins and knuckle busters, not to mention the deadly and infamous Long Nap, and will employ them against the Special Interests. I am no smarter than anybody else and I don't claim to have all the answers but it ain't nuclear physics and I will work hard and accept no special

privileges and what I don't know about state government, I'll know a month after I take office."

My platform was exactly as follows:

1. I will not tell a lie.
2. I make no promise except to do my best.
3. Any tax surplus goes straight back to you the folks.
4. I will scorn big business and Special Interests in favor of you the taxpayer and voter. The trough is closed.
5. There will be action, not just a lot of yik-yakking.
6. No weenies need apply.
7. Let's party.

Career politicians like to act like government is the **Mystery of Mysteries,** unknowable except to the Grand Poobahs of the Sacred Elect. Well, I came out of the weeds to beat a weaselly Democrat and a wascally Wepublican who each thought he was a great statesman and I was the idiot with the hump, and **on Election Day I ate their lunch.**

I destroyed my opponents in the televised debates. I hung them out to dry.

The weaselly Democrat talked about government's needing to create jobs. I said, "There used to be a country for people like you but it doesn't exist anymore. Its capital was **Moscow."**

He whimpered and looked toward the corner of the studio, where his advisers and pollsters were standing, holding his cue cards. They were helpless to save him.

The Wepublican was a scrawny runt with one wet finger in the wind who used the word "family" in every sentence, as if this might win him an Amana gas range, and said he favored social welfare programs if they "strengthened the family." I leaned forward and let him have it.

"I said, "You flat-headed fisheyed sap-sucking belly scratcher. All you do is bark when the big boys yank your chain."

I said, "If a person is smart enough to live in Minnesota, then he is smart enough to take care of his own self and not look around for a handout."

Nobody else dared to say it plain like that.

And in gratitude, the people of Minnesota put me in the governor's office.

Arnold called my suite at the Lucky Lucre at 11 P.M. on Election Night and I let the machine pick up. It was a thrill to hear his voice say "Jimmy? Jimmy, are you there? If you're there, pick up, Jimmy. It's Arnold. Let me give you my cell-phone number."

He never gave me his private number before.

I called him awhile later and he congratulated me and asked, "What can I do for you?"

I said, "Go back and find that *Strong Man* script and read it and see if it wouldn't be perfect for me."

He said, "You're going to be pretty busy for the next four years, pal."

I told him I would have plenty of time to make a movie, being an advocate of less government, not more, and that I was keeping myself in shape for it. I asked him, "Arnold, did you use a body double in your last movie—I forget the title—you know, that comedy that tanked?"

I had fun with him. It was the first time in my life Arnold Schwarzenegger ever called me up on the telephone.

 I was sworn in on Monday, January 4, and the national press was fawning all over me. *Newsweek*, *Time*, you name it. **Al Gore** phoned that morning and wished me luck. "Thanks, Al," I said. "See you in Iowa." He had a coughing fit. We had a fabulous inaugural ball at the Civic Center, at which I appeared at one end of the arena, in a spotlight, standing on a tiny platform a hundred feet in the air, and lowered myself hand over hand down a length of barbed wire to the stage, where I stripped to the waist and bench-pressed 400 pounds and then Robert Plant and some blues bands played for five hours and we sold 30,000 gallons of *Jimmy Big Boy* beer and 12,000 *Love the Gov* T-shirts.

I'd like to see any governor match me for merchandise sales.

And the next day I drove to the capitol and walked into the governor's office. I walked across a carpet that felt like a marsh and sat down behind a desk the size of a rowboat and looked around at the plush chairs, the oil painting of the first territorial legislature in their top hats and waistcoats and fringed epaulets, the gilded gewgaws and stuffed birds and a marble bust of Henry Sibley and vases and glass cases,

and in walks a guy in a brown suit and a tie with designer ameba on it and shoes with tassels who introduces himself as my chief of staff. I said, "Whoever you are, get this crap out of here. This is not an operetta. This is the office of the people's governor. And what is this rose doing here on my desk?" **A single long-stemmed rose,** with a note: **"Wemembel me when the canderights ah greaming."**

CHAPTER 24

2000

Al Gore, look out. Fame is a fickle lady. Guys like you who chase her hard never lay a hand on her and guys like me who act like she doesn't exist, we are the guys she loves. Right now she is nuts about me.

You're obsolete, Al. The fringe is the center now. TV has made a joke of politics and a joker like me can beat a stuffed owl like you. You are living in the nineteenth century when the president stood at a lectern and read a speech in a big pipe-organ voice and everyone listened and nobody's dog barked. Those days are gone.

And you are disadvantaged by being **Bill's Best Friend.**

Bill Clinton was building his legacy and then he committed indiscretions with a certain starstruck intern. If he'd

had a spoonful of brains, he'd have come out to the Rose Garden on a Saturday afternoon as the sun set and confessed to the whole affair in writing and after one week of people's pooping on him, it would have been over and done, good-bye. Instead, he consulted his idiot lawyers, who got him into a hide-and-seek game, and TV zeroed in on him like a hawk on a field mouse. TV abhors full disclosure in writing and loves suspense. TV doesn't care about the law or the Constitution, but it's happy to spend months standing on the White House drive and staring at Bill and asking, "Is he lying? Could someone that smart really be that dumb?"

So TV took a little indiscretion and with Bill's help turned it into the **Crime of the Century.** He was the Not Too Bright Guy and you are his roommate.

I've told the truth in this book and held nothing back. I want to focus on the future, not the past.

I have appointed Earl Woofner and other great minds to run Minnesota day to day and give me monthly briefings, either in person or by telephone or fax. I have instructed the Highway Patrol to stop The **Rodent**'s car and find enough deadly reefer in the trunk to send him up the river for three hundred years. Then I will get myself in fighting trim and complete my deal to fight **Mr. Mashimoto Ishi** for six million dollars, and I will run for president.

Jimmy (Big Boy) Valente,
Governor of Minnesota
versus
Mashimoto Ishi, the 800-pound
Emperor of the East
Best Out of Three Falls, No Time Limit, No Holds
Barred, No Medical Assistance Permitted. The Ring to Be
Surrounded by Blazing Gasoline and Accordion Wire.
LIMIT OF THREE CRUISE MISSILES PER WRESTLER.

Mashimoto, the sumo king of Hokkaido, a mound of flesh the size of a compact car and quick as a cat, with an ugly Kabuki mug like an overripe pumpkin. He leans on you and you feel your bones bend, your vertebrae compress, your synapses snap shut. He eats a ferocious fermented cabbage concoction at ringside and clambers into the ring and does his bows and the salt toss, then gets you in a clinch and breathes on you and you sneeze about sixteen times and then he spits on his hands and rubs them in your eyes and it burns like acid and you fall, twitching, convulsive, dazed, to the mat, another Yankee casualty of kim chee.

I fought him at the **Cow Palace** in **San Francisco** and he was disqualified on a technicality for busting a folding chair over my head when I had been hurled out of the ring and lay facedown on the press table, my eyeballs stuck to a sports-writer's bismarck.

We had a rematch at **Long Beach,** and Mashimoto and I stood toe to toe, slashing and scratching, and the match was called on account of the referee's fainting from the blood.

Our second rematch in **Atlantic City** was canceled after

Mashimoto ran into the ropes intending to bounce off and hit me with a General Tsao's Eight Celestial Joys Flying Calamari and instead he took the ropes with him and landed in the second row and sprained his ankle.

The third rematch is scheduled for July Fourth at **Caesar's Palace,** and the contract is 98 percent a done deal. All that's left to decide is ancillary rights and whether Felix and Mashimoto and I can agree on a script. Felix thinks a Jap TKO of an incumbent U.S. governor would set up a "firestorm" fourth rematch. And he wants me to wear bib overalls and lead a pig on a rope and sing "The She's-Too-Fat Polka." I told him, "Felix, this is the biggest purse in the history of pro wrestling, ten million bucks. Plenty for everyone. I will pin him and blow him up with plastics, and we can schedule the fourth rematch for two days before the California primary."

The six-million-dollar share I earn from crushing the evil Jap is what will finance my presidential campaign against that **cigar-store Indian Al Gore** and enable me to whip his skinny ass in **New Hampshire** and **Iowa.** I look forward to it. Two independent states full of notoriously cranky voters who delight in depantsing the anointed front-runner and sending his gravy train onto a sidetrack. When Al garners 8 percent of the vote in **New Hampshire,** compared to 52 percent for the wild-card candidate with the big pink noggin, I am going to enjoy watching him go on TV to explain what happened, like someone explaining why his car went in the ditch on a bright summer day.

Six million dollars in a presidential campaign is bird feed but I will win with it because I am the underdog and Al will be the 10–1 favorite and when he crashes he will crumble. He will wind up running the **Ford Foundation** and chairing conferences on the future of international exchange programs and I will be a president you can be proud of and land in *Air Force One* and inspect honor guards and do my duty and none of that groping in the West Wing. I will do mine upstairs in the First Bedroom. What I don't know about being president, I will learn. I don't have time to fail.

And when my chief of staff walks into the **OVAL OFFICE** and says, "Arnold Schwarzenegger is here to see you, Mr. President," I will tend to a few other things before buzzing Arnold in. I will maybe order a tuna sandwich and a glass of skim milk and place a phone call to Svend and ask how the grass is growing in Jimmyville and perhaps get a weather forecast, maybe check the sports scores. And then when Arnold walks in and gives me his big grin and pumps my hand, I'll say, **"I wish I had more time for you, pal, but it's one of those days. I've got prime ministers and premiers backed up from here to the hall closet."** Maybe I won't offer him a chair, just stand in the middle of the room, hands in my pockets and look over his shoulder toward the door, and when he leans close and says, "How about the ambassadorship to Austria?" I'll say, "How about Monaco? The work isn't so hard and you're closer to the beach."

You gotta love it.

GHOST:

Are we done now?

I'm not, but you are. Type it up and print it.

GHOST:

Shall we send you a copy?

Don't need one. It's my life. I lived it. Why would I want to waste time reading about it?

GHOST:

Something is moving behind that curtain.

All I would add is: It's going to happen. I can visualize it. It's as real to me as those surfers on the horizon, against the pellucid sky, riding to the shore. I can do it standing or sitting, either way I'm going to land on the beach. You—

GHOST:

Jimmy? Jimmy, what happened? Are you all right?

I feel funny. Have I been saying weird things?

GHOST:

Those two little red marks on your neck—did something bite you?

I have this funny feeling that maybe I said something wrong. Could I listen to the tapes? I don't want to offend anybody.

GHOST:

Thank you, Governor.